HOSTILE, BUT DEAD

On top of each table lay a figure covered with a sheet. As Hammond, O'Neill, and Samuels looked on, the CMO pulled the sheet off one of them, revealing a naked male body bearing the marks of high-powered gunshot wounds.

Aside from the evidence of cause of death, the body was marked by what looked like metal embedded in the forehead: an encircled oval containing a snakelike squiggle, and an X-shaped slit in his belly. The slit didn't appear to be a wound; it looked as if it was either a natural opening or one the body had carried for a long, long time.

"Anyone you know, Colonel?" Hammond challenged. O'Neill just stared at him. Apparently retired colonels didn't have to answer rhetorical questions.

"They're not human," the doctor offered.

"You think?" O'Neill said, simulating amazement. It was probably a good thing this guy was still technically a civilian, Samuels thought. The word *smart-ass* came irresistibly to mind.

D0173830

STARGATE SG-1

Ashley McConnell

A ROC BOOK

ROC
Published by New American Library, a division of
Penguin Group (USA) Inc., 375 Hudson Street,
New York, New York 10014, USA
Penguin Group (Canada), 10 Alcorn Avenue, Toronto,
Ontario M4V 3B2, Canada (a division of Pearson Penguin Canada Inc.)
Penguin Books Ltd., 80 Strand, London WC2R 0RL, England
Penguin Ireland, 25 St. Stephen's Green, Dublin 2,
Ireland (a division of Penguin Books Ltd.)
Penguin Group (Australia), 250 Camberwell Road, Camberwell, Victoria 3124,
Australia (a division of Pearson Australia Group Pty. Ltd.)
Penguin Books India Pvt. Ltd., 11 Community Centre, Panchsheel Park,
New Delhi - 110 017, India
Penguin Group (NZ), Cnr Airborne and Rosedale Roads, Albany,
Auckland 1310, New Zealand (a division of Pearson New Zealand Ltd.)
Penguin Books (South Africa) (Pty.) Ltd., 24 Sturdee Avenue,
Rosebank, Johannesburg 2196, South Africa

Penguin Books Ltd., Registered Offices:
80 Strand, London WC2R 0RL, England

First published by Roc, an imprint of New American Library,
a division of Penguin Group (USA) Inc.

First Printing, October 1998
10   9   8   7   6   5   4   3   2

Copyright © Metro Goldwyn Mayer, 1998
All rights reserved

ROC REGISTERED TRADEMARK—MARCA REGISTRADA

Printed in the United States of America

PUBLISHER'S NOTE
This is a work of fiction. Names, characters, places, and incidents either are
the product of the author's imagination or are used fictitiously, and any resemblance to actual persons, living or dead, business establishments, events, or
locales is entirely coincidental.

ACKNOWLEDGMENTS

Special thanks to Laura Anne Gilman, Jennifer Jackson, and Sue Phillips, without whom, etc. Particular thanks to the producers of STARGATE SG-1, who were kind enough to provide substantial background material which made the conversion of a script to this novel that much easier. And, of course, to Jonathan Glassner and Brad Wright, whose script it was to begin with. I hope I managed to do it justice.

STARGATE SG-1

CHAPTER ONE

The room was twenty-eight stories deep in the guts of a mountain, and it was damned cold.

Cold, dark, and sitrep boring.

The world over, the military does things like that: hiding important installations under tons of granite, hoping nothing and no one can find them, and if someone does happen to trip over the sensors and razor wire, and then get past all the armed guards, that the enemy will somehow still be prevented from getting in by the sheer weight of all that granite.

Sometimes the military buries things in mountains that they don't want getting *out*.

Either way, the room buried in the mountain, the reason for all the security and all the burrows and rooms around it, was huge: three stories tall. It swallowed light, as if concrete and steel absorbed the radiation somehow and reflected nothing back. The room was filled with equipment, consoles and dumb terminals, but they were all shrouded in tarps and plastic to protect them against dust.

At one end of the room a huge shape, flat and round like a pancake set on end, focused the eye; at the other, an observation-room window took up most of the wall. A shallow steel-grid ramp led up to the tarp-covered disk. Ramp and disk were set off from the rest of the room by a wide-painted border of yellow and black stripes alternating with the legend KEEP CLEAR.

Looking up, through the window of the observation deck, one could see all the ghostly, shrouded shapes of a briefing room, table, chairs, overhead projector, videoconferencing setup. There was even an automatic whiteboard, one of those with a magic button to press so a scanning bar passing over its surface would transfer any written information to a piece of glossy paper extruding from one side. But they were only shapes covered with translucent plastic, abandoned. No one had held a briefing there in quite some time.

The only sounds in the room were the whining of a dying fluorescent light and the voices, not enough to fill so much cubic space.

The folding table set up at the foot of the ramp overlapped the painted border, as if its warning had lost its meaning over time. The five human beings sitting around a folding table not far from the foot of the ramp were highly trained professional military security personnel, one woman and four men with squeaky-clean backgrounds and the most specialized security clearances in-depth investigations could give them. They were veterans. Experienced. Sharp.

Bored.

Playing poker.

Their weapons, military-issue semiautomatic rifles, were piled up along the wall, near the exit, out of reach. The guards, twenty-eight stories deep inside a mountain, where not even a thermonuclear bomb could reach them, propped their feet on the table and chewed cigars. They'd been on this tour too long, and there was money on the table. They'd been doing this forever.

Except one: the woman. Sergeant Carol Ketering, young, blonde, still gung-ho. She was new to this assignment, and uneasy about the looming circle of drapes at the top of the ramp. She kept looking around, waiting for someone to comment about how quiet it was. Too quiet.

But then you didn't get much noise down this far. The guts of a mountain rarely gurgle.

Sergeant Keithley, unconcerned, slapped a final round of cards around the table. Even his voice was bored.

"Everybody anted up? Seven to the deuce, nothing there. Eight, nothing happening. King gets a queen—possible straight. Eight on the eight. And jack gets a boss. Eights open." Keithley flicked a glance at the new kid, then went back to the cards.

She wasn't really paying attention to the game, which meant she'd get cleaned out sooner rather than later. But Ketering was the kind with more sense than to bet her last dollar. Lots of good sense. So why was she spooked?

Ketering was getting even more nervous, as

if the room was too big. She jerked her head around, as if trying to catch sight of something too quick to see.

"Aren't you guys afraid of an officer coming down here or something?" She tried hard to sound insouciant. A couple of players exchanged smiles. She really wanted to be one of the guys, didn't she?

"Trust me, nobody ever comes down here but us," one of the others responded.

She wasn't reassured, somehow. The disk, beneath the tarps, was . . . vibrating? The tarps seemed to billow, as if stirred by some breeze.

"Does that thing always do that?" she demanded, her voice high and sharp.

"Do what?" Keithley was getting annoyed. Ketering was interrupting the game, and the only interesting thing about this damned duty was the poker game. There was certainly nothing interesting about the big disk.

"Whatever that thing is under the tarp. I just saw it move or do something. . . ."

"Probably the only thing it ever did was cost money," Airman Liverakos observed sourly, swiveling a cigar around the words.

Keithley, examining his cards, grunted derisively. "Looks like they ran out. They've been shipping personnel out of here for months." Maybe once this place was shut down for good they'd be assigned someplace interesting.

"Whatever." Liverakos shrugged. "You in or out?" he asked Ketering.

The dust in the air, a sign of poorly maintained air filters, danced in the dim light. Trembled.

"I'm telling you, it looks like it's moving."

The guards laughed. Trust a woman's vivid imagination! But her fancies were still interrupting the game, and Liverakos added, "If you don't have the straight, just fold."

Ketering was no longer pretending to pay attention to the game. Rising from her chair, she started up the ramp slowly, hesitantly. Her combat boots rang hollowly on the metal grid.

The other four squad members watched her curiously.

"Can we take that as a fold?" Liverakos asked.

At the top of the ramp she paused. There was a distinct fluttering sound now as the tarp draped over the disk rippled against the ropes keeping it in place.

By this time Ketering and the disk had the full attention of the other four guards; the money and cards on the table were almost forgotten.

"Whoa!" Keithley yelled as the ashtrays on the table began stuttering to the edge, to the concrete floor. One crashed into a million splinters.

The vibration was real and it was loud. The guards rose to their feet as the rumble increased, staring at the huge cloth-covered shape at the top of the ramp. The splinters danced.

Abruptly the sitrep changed: DEFCON ONE.

The tarps ripped away from the disk as if blown off in a hurricane. The cloth slapped into the walls, but the guards ignored it, fascinated by the hidden disk finally revealed and by the monstrous storm contained in its—empty?—center.

Supported by side buttresses, the disk looked like two concentric stone circles, divided into sections, each section engraved with its own enigmatic symbol. But unlike any stone monument any of them had ever seen, this one seemed alive. The inner ring was moving, like the circle of a combination lock. Acting according to its own mysterious logic, it spun back and forth. Each time it stopped, a V-shaped section of the outer ring seemed to snap into place, and the strange symbol under the locked section glowed.

The guards, dazed but professional, scrambled for the neglected weapons. As Ketering dived to join them, she commented breathlessly, "I take it this never happened before. . . ."

Liverakos lunged for a red phone on the wall. The whole room, three stories high, was shaking. The noise of the vibration kept getting louder, louder than jet engines, than earthquakes. The bones of the mountain were grinding together. The soldiers crouched, armed, staring at the artifact that had suddenly developed a mind of its own, had come alive before their very eyes. This was much less boring than the poker game. Their breath came short, shallow; their eyes were wide, fingers damp on their rifles.

And then, with a roar even louder than the vibrating mountain, something bright, something between light and water and yet both at once, gushed out from the center of the circles, a funnel like a horizontal whirlpool lancing through the air over their heads, taller than any of them at its origin. They scattered, belly down; Liverakos, shouting into the red phone, abandoned it, hitting the deck with the rest of them. The funnel of shaped light ignored them, snapping back into the disk, shimmering over the previously empty surface like sunlight on lake water.

And then there was silence.

The absence of noise was almost painful.

"Anybody got any ideas?" Keithley said, his voice shaking. The rest of them cowered, remembering the first law of the military: Never volunteer. Especially not for something like this.

But Ketering was too young perhaps, too new to know that law. As the others watched, appalled, she got up, staring at the vertical pool of light as if entranced, and walked slowly up the ramp again, her rifle in her hand.

"What the hell are you doing?" someone yelled, not unreasonably.

Fascinated, she lifted a hand to touch the glittering surface.

As if in response, a metal sphere the size of a softball bounced out of the opaque light. Startled, Ketering stepped back, and then stooped to pick it up, turning it around in her hands.

"What're you doing!"

"Don't touch it!"

As if the sphere were a flashlight her touch had activated, a cone of light sprang out of it and drenched her face in a pink glow.

"It's beautiful . . ." she murmured, and turned to the other guards, as if inviting them to share something precious—

And the Monster jumped out and grabbed her.

Or at least so it seemed to the stunned guards, as a figure at least seven feet tall stepped through the shimmering curtain, disarming Ketering and using her as a shield with what seemed to be one smooth motion. The figure had the head of a gray king cobra, hood flared; it looked like the giant economy size of the uraeus, the snake symbol on the crowns of ancient Egypt. The figure wore heavy boots, a tunic that looked like chain mail covered by a broad, flat collar, and a skirt that looked like a kilt. It carried a six-foot thick-headed staff, holding it by a grip in the middle. The staff had a broad, thick, flat leaf shape on one end.

The guards barely had time to register that the "head" of the serpent thing was actually a helmet, with broad overlapping "neck" plates where a human being's face would be, when it was followed by five more, who immediately deployed in a narrow semicircle on the metal ramp. The human guards were aiming at what was clearly a line of defense for the next to come through the disk, their leader. They held their staffs at the ready, as if they were weapons.

He too was wearing a serpent helmet, this one in gold, its eyes bright red jewels. His collar was even broader and encrusted with turquoise, amethyst, onyx, rubies. He was of medium height, not as tall as his escort or as heavily muscled, but he was the focus of all attention. As he stepped clear of the curtain, it disappeared, as if shutting down, and finally there was a long moment of pure silence in the room as the golden serpent's head swiveled back and forth.

And then the serpent's head flipped upward,

as the neck plates folded into themselves, into the golden collar, and the Air Force guards could see the human face of the intruder. And human it was, dark, young, the smooth, clear face of a man who had never known an imperfection, never suffered a flaw. His skull was covered by a tightly fitting gold cap. His expression was cold, impassive. His eyes were dark, heavily lined with kohl. He saw the woman, still held by his chief bodyguard.

His eyes were hot.

Glowing, like a furnace.

"Jaafa! Kree!"

The words were commands to his escort, the squad could tell. The gray serpent head of the one immediately next to him flipped up as well, the overlapping scales of the neck plates sliding into one another, until the guards could see his face. He looked human too, African perhaps or African-American, a large, solid man. On his forehead was a golden symbol, an oval lying on its side containing a serpentine line, the whole nearly encircled by yet another line. His strong features were emphasized by the closely fitting skullcap he wore, a duller gray version of the one worn by the leader.

"Teal'c! Kree!" his commander repeated, clearly impatient. This time it was addressed directly to the one who held Ketering. For an instant the black man looked at the golden one, as if wondering at the command. He looked curiously for a moment at her M–16 and then at the similar weapons aimed at him by her squad mates. It was clear that he had never seen a rifle before. It was equally clear that he recognized the threat.

Still, the order registered, and the bodyguard tossed the weapon aside as if it were nothing but a toy, and pushed the struggling woman into the other's arms.

"Get your hands *off* . . ." Ketering gasped, still fighting, but her struggles availed her nothing. The leader placed his open hand on her forehead. The alien's forearm was wrapped in a metallic ribbon, curling around the wrist, webbing over the palm, terminating in rings on each finger and sheaths for each fingertip. The ribbon bound red stones to both the back of the hand and the palm.

The palm stone glowed red. Pulses of visible energy flowed through the ribbon. She sagged, her resistance overcome even though her eyes were still open.

"Let her go!" Keithley yelled.

The golden alien brushed over the scene with contempt. *"Jaafa! Mol kek!"*

In response, his bodyguard pointed their staffs at the squad. The thick, bulbous leaf heads of the staffs split lengthwise like the gaping jaws of alligators, hummed savagely, and flung bolts of energy that turned a section of concrete wall into dust.

The squad dived for what cover there was and returned fire, but their bullets had no effect. The golden leader studied his passive captive, his perfect face widening into an evil smile, as if the deadly rifle fire richocheting around him was of no more importance than a refreshing mist. His fingertips brushed her cheek, lifted a lock of her blond hair. Ketering stared up at him, as if dreaming.

Liverakos fell back and used a shrouded console as cover to get to the red emergency phone, yelling into it, "This is Area C! We're under heavy fire down here! Area C! Need—"

A bolt from another alien staff caught him squarely in the chest, and a clean hole a foot in diameter appeared beneath the arch of his ribs. He slid to the floor, mouth still working, dead before he knew what hit him. The phone dangled from the wall, a tinny voice squawking out of the receiver.

Keithley cursed and stood, firing steadily until another bolt of energy sheared him in half.

Teal'c, the chief bodyguard, watched, letting the others do the fighting; his job, clearly, was to protect the golden one. His leader handed him Ketering to carry, as if she were a doll, weightless.

The two remaining members of the human squad continued firing, retreating behind consoles and desks. As if they had rehearsed the tactic, they concentrated their fire on the two bodyguards in the front, nearest them. Pieces of the alien armor were chipped away by bullets even as the walls and the shelter the humans used were blasted in return. But eventually the focused fire reached alien flesh, and the first two serpent-headed aliens fell.

The two men wasted no time in cries of triumph; they focused on the next two serpent-headed guards, unable to get a clear shot at the leader and unwilling to aim for the one who held Ketering.

The fall of two of his escorts finally pulled the attention of the leader from his captive. This was not, obviously, according to expectation. Enraged, the golden one finally realized that these humans he viewed with such contempt actually presented a real threat. *"Kreeka! Jaafa!"* he cried.

As he did so, the disk behind him began to rumble once again, as the strange power energized it.

The remaining bodyguards opened fire. One man died instantly under the lashing flares of energy bolts. The last man left free and alive scrabbled desperately for the door to the room, attempting to open the locks. He had no cover, no shield from the converging flares of power. He was dead before he saw them hit.

Only Carol Ketering was left to be human witness as the stomach plates in the armor of the two dead aliens opened, as white, foot-long creatures snaked their way out into the air. She was the only human witness, but what she saw did not register in her face or in her eyes. Helpless in the grip of the chief bodyguard, she saw without seeing.

The two white worms launched themselves through the air to the hands of the golden leader, who welcomed them with open arms and coos of sympathy. As he soothed them, he reached down and recovered the sphere that had been the first object through the disk. He paid no attention at all to the abandoned bodies of his slain escort.

Finished with their slaughter, the remaining serpent-headed guards began to pass back through the shimmering opening.

Only the leader, the bodyguard, and their captive were left when the rescue party burst through the now unlocked door. Twenty soldiers fanned out, weapons ready, followed by a man in a general's uniform.

The general's face registered the horror of the battleground, the golden lord, his companion, and his helpless captive. He snapped a command to hold fire.

The golden one merely looked at him. As he did so, the whites of his eyes began to glow like white fire, turning the dark irises into pits from hell. Sneering, he turned away and stepped through the shimmer of the gate, his escort behind him. As soon as they did, the shimmer vanished, and the disk was silent and empty.

The human military looked around the room, seeing their dead, seeing the alien dead. Pools of fire still crackled where energy bolts had hit. The poker table, flipped over, its legs vulnerable in the air, had a gaping hole in the center where someone had tried and failed to use it as a shield.

Twenty-eight stories deep inside a mountain, it was cold.

Deep inside the heart of General George Hammond, it was colder still, with the knowledge that the Stargate was in use once again.

CHAPTER TWO

Major Bert Samuels checked his watch as they made the final turn onto the quiet street. Just past midnight—not bad for a medium-long drive from the base.

They were in a quiet residential area, well established judging by the landscaping. Not many lights interrupted the velvet darkness of the sky—reasonable figuring how late it was. He hoped the man he was looking for was still up. If not, well, that would be just his luck, dammit. He'd be up once Samuels got through with him.

His driver slowed, creeping along, looking for some sign of numbers on the discreet driveways or the mailboxes, half-hidden by shrubbery. Samuels bit back an irritated remark. He wanted to get this over with, get home, and wrap himself around a drink. He was an officer, not an errand boy.

Well, unless he was outranked. As a mere major that happened more often than he really liked. He thought once he'd made it past captain he'd have it made, but now instead of majors making his life miserable, it was generals. And colonels. But it was part of the game, and playing the game got you promoted until you were finally the one who got to send junior officers on errands like this one. Samuels was looking forward to that day nearly as much as he was looking forward to getting home. Not that getting home anytime soon was on the agenda for the foreseeable future.

The car pulled into the drive and jolted to a stop. Samuels got out, followed by the driver.

"This is it?"

"Yes, sir." The driver, an airman, was required to be polite even in the face of stupid questions.

The house at the end of the long walkway was dark and silent, with only a single, discreetly shaded light gleaming on the porch.

The place looked deserted, and it was cold enough that he wished he'd brought a coat. Samuels sighed. There would be hell to pay if he didn't bring back his man as ordered. The two men started toward the front door, Samuels smoothing the wrinkles out of his uniform jacket and replacing his hat on his head as he went. It never hurt to look sharp.

At least there were lights on in the house. He could glimpse a living room through the flimsy drapes, a stone fireplace mantel. But there was no sign of the man he was seeking.

He lifted the door knocker, applied it briskly. They waited. Nothing happened.

"If he's not here . . ." the officer muttered.

"I thought I saw someone on the roof when we pulled into the drive, sir," the driver suggested, not quite diffidently.

"Why would he be on the roof?" Samuels demanded.

The driver knew better than to try to answer that one. He pointed at the side of the house. "There's a ladder over there."

Samuels cursed under his breath. Climbing ladders in the dark? With his luck the house would be alarmed, and he'd find himself arrested, and wouldn't *that* look good on his personnel jacket. . . .

Orders were orders. Up he went, mentally daring the airman waiting below to say anything more. The enlisted man, wise to the ways of not-yet-senior career officers, kept his mouth shut. He might have been smirking, but Samuels couldn't tell.

The roof was peaked on one side of the house, flat on the other. Samuels brushed himself off again and looked around.

The isolation of the area meant there wasn't much light pollution, and a glance at the sky nearly took the captain's breath away—he'd never appreciated how *many* stars there were out there. It took a few seconds to realize that there was someone else on the roof, sitting over a telescope, also looking at the stars.

"Colonel Jack O'Neill?" Samuels asked, suddenly uncertain. He was at an angle to the other man, and got an impression of quiet scruff—something like a college professor perhaps, if college professors went in for black leather jackets, black T-shirts, and khaki pants.

O'Neill looked tall, even seated, with light hair—the kind of blond that didn't show gray—and Samuels would bet his flight pay he'd never had any trouble meeting fitness requirements. He appeared to be in his forties, young to be retired. But O'Neill was far more involved with what he was seeing in the eyepiece than in any visitors who might climb up into his refuge.

"Retired," O'Neill answered, not looking up. *Go away* hung heavy in the air.

The other man swallowed. "I'm Major Samuels."

"Air Force?" O'Neill asked absently, still not looking up.

Samuels swallowed again. "Yes, sir." O'Neill might not look like it, he might be retired, but he still had rank, even if it was only by courtesy. He had presence too. Samuels found himself fighting an urge to stand to attention. He really didn't like that. "I'm the general's executive officer." So *there.*

O'Neill lifted his head at last, away from the eyepiece, but only to look at the millions of glittering lights in the sky directly. The revelation of Samuels' exalted position clearly failed to impress him.

"Want a piece of advice?" O'Neill said conversationally. "Try to get re-assed to NASA. That's where the action's going to be." He waved his hand at the glory of the stars over their heads. "Out there."

Samuels reminded himself he hadn't come for career counseling and took a deep breath. "I, um, I'm under orders to bring you to see General Hammond."

O'Neill, still staring at the sky, said dismissively, "Never heard of him."

Oh, hell. "He replaced General *West*, sir." *You do remember General West, I hope?*

There was a short silence. Then O'Neill sighed, turning back to the telescope and fiddling with a small knob. "Well, I'm a busy man, Major."

Clearly, this was not going to be a career-enhancing assignment unless something drastic happened. Samuels took a deep breath. He'd been authorized to say this outside the confines of the base, but only if he really had to. It looked very much like he had to.

"I can see that, sir. He says it's important. It

has to do with . . ."—*Use the exact words, Major*—" 'the Stargate.' "

The moment froze, as if caught in a frame of film. Then O'Neill turned toward him, the telescope finally forgotten, and looked him directly in the eye.

Samuels swallowed again, and hoped he would never in his life have cause to have a look like that one on his face.

O'Neill had barely spoken during the entire trip to the base. Samuels had tried once or twice to make conversation, but O'Neill ignored him, staring out the windows into the darkness, up at the sky. He seemed to be pulled deep into himself, thinking—remembering maybe.

The base was on full alert. Samuels watched O'Neill covertly as the other man noted the automatic vehicle gate, backed up by armed sentries; second and third checkpoints; airmen patrolling the roofs of the cinder-block buildings surrounding the entry tucked under the granite overhang of the mountain. Both Samuels and his driver had to show identification repeatedly until the vehicle was parked and they entered the main facility.

They walked past more sentries carrying both sidearms and rifles, down a long hallway, and into a steel elevator. The driver left them there. Samuels kept watching, looking for some sign of emotion in the other man's face. But since that single flash of—something—in O'Neill's eyes at the mention of the Stargate, there was nothing. He might have been strolling through the local mall.

At Sublevel Eleven they left the elevator and walked down another hallway. Pausing before a reception desk, Samuels said, "We'll have to take another elevator. It's a long way down."

The corner of O'Neill's mouth twitched. "I know," he said, reaching for a clipboard and signing it. "I've been here before."

Chagrined, Samuels muttered an acknowledgment. On the way down this time he faced the front of the elevator, standing at parade rest.

Of course O'Neill was no stranger to the base. He didn't even blink at the guards, the fences, the elevators that plunged them deep into the mountain. He knew where they were going without being told, allowing Samuels to lead him through the halls. They turned a last corner and confronted one last guard who announced their arrival with a "This way, sir."

"Come." The voice from within was gruff and weary.

Samuels came to attention in front of the large desk, snapping a salute. Hammond looked up from the file he was reading and returned it.

"General Hammond: Colonel Jack O'Neill."

"Retired," O'Neill added.

Hammond looked him over as Samuel stepped back. O'Neill, still unimpressed, looked right back. Samuels found himself anticipating this interview more than he'd expected to. He'd read the reports, of course, synopsized them for Hammond—that was part of completed staff work. The reports told him all about the first Stargate mission, not enough about O'Neill. Who was this guy? Why had he retired early? And why, in the midst of more than top secret base lockdown had Hammond insisted on summoning him? Had the general seen more in the files than Samuels had?

"I can see that," Hammond agreed, looking over the casual stance, the leather jacket, the hint that O'Neill might have skipped shaving. O'Neill had made no effort to come to attention, though there was tension in the broad shoulders that suggested he might be fighting the inclination. Old habits died hard, even in retirees.

"I envy you, Colonel," Hammond went on.

"Sir?" O'Neill inquired neutrally. Samuels hid a smirk. He knew that give-no-opening tone; he'd used it to superior officers himself a time or two. It was the military version of wide-eyed innocence.

"For retiring," Hammond answered. "Me, I'm on my last tour." He set down the file. "Time to start getting my thoughts together, maybe write a book. You ever think of writing a book about your exploits in the line of duty?"

Exploits? Samuels thought. The Stargate mission qualified as an "exploit"? It wasn't a word he would have chosen. But then, he wouldn't have thought Hammond, a solid, by-the-book crusty career man, would play games. He was about as ready to retire, Samuels thought, as the man in the moon. Hammond's whole life was the Air Force and service to his county.

"Thought about it," O'Neill said laconically. "But then I'd have to shoot anyone who actually read it."

Hammond stared at O'Neill a moment, weighing the possibility of insubordination. Samuels nearly choked. The general was also crafty, cunning, and sharp, and didn't tolerate fools.

"That's a joke, sir. Most of my work the past ten years was classified," O'Neill went on, explaining the obvious. He'd be hell on wheels to work for if you got on his wrong side, Samuels decided, and thanked God he reported directly to Hammond. Hammond didn't do wry.

"Oh. Yes, of course."

The tall man in the leather jacket took a deep breath, clearly deciding to cut through the bull. "Major Samuels mentioned something about the Stargate."

Hammond nodded, acknowledging. "Down

to business. I can do that. This way." He stood, brushed past the other men to lead the way out of the office. Samuels followed. He hadn't been invited, exactly, but they hadn't told him to leave either, and he had a good idea where they were going next. Besides, he was Hammond's XO, and where Hammond went he was going to follow.

He was right. A few minutes later, wending their way through more steel tunnels, stepping around suddenly activated hordes of maintenance personnel-replacing light bulbs and checking electrical boxes, they were in the base infirmary. Normally this place saw nothing more serious than tetanus shots or annual physical exams; broken bones were a big deal here.

Lately something far more serious than broken bones had claimed the attention of the medical officer; the infirmary had been turned into a combination of morgue and pathology lab. In the middle of what used to be an exam room were several stainless steel gurneys with funnels down the side. Samuels didn't want to think about what the grooves were meant to channel away.

On top of each table lay a figure covered with a sheet. As Hammond, O'Neill, and Samuels looked on, the CMO pulled the sheet off one of them, revealing a naked male body bearing the marks of high-powered gunshot wounds.

Aside from the evidence of cause of death, the body was marked by what looked like metal embedded in the forehead—an encircled oval containing a snakelike squiggle—and an X-shaped slit in his belly. The slit didn't appear to be a wound; it looked as if it was either a natural opening, or one the body had carried for a long, long time.

"Anyone you know, Colonel?" Hammond challenged. O'Neill just stared at him. Apparently retired colonels didn't have to answer rhetorical questions.

"They're not human," the doctor offered.

"You think?" O'Neill said, simulating amazement. It was probably a good thing this guy was still technically a civilian, Samuels thought. The word "smart-ass" came irresistibly to mind.

The doctor ignored the sarcasm. "Best we

can tell, these slits are actually a pouch similar to that found on a marsupial."

"Like a kangaroo," Samuels supplemented, eager to add his own two cents. O'Neill gave him a glance that made it quite clear he hadn't required a supplementary explanation.

"Except in both sexes," the doctor went on, pulling a sheet off another gurney. This one was obviously female. She too bore the forehead marks and the X-shaped pouch.

"These people, or aliens, or whatever you want to call them, came through and killed four of my people and kidnapped another using advanced weapons," Hammond said heavily.

O'Neill's head came up a fraction, like a war horse hearing a distant trumpet. "Weapons, sir?"

The general turned to a staff propped against the wall, picked it up, and showed it to the other man.

Samuels blurted, "We can't figure out how they opera—"

It was clear that O'Neill had seen it before. He took the staff and slid his hand down one side in a practiced motion, almost as if he were cocking a shotgun, uncovered a lever and flicked it. The bulb end of the staff popped open, lightning sizzling between its jaws, ready to fire. Everyone else in the room stepped hurriedly back.

"Seen one before, I take it?" Hammond said hollowly.

O'Neill took a deep breath, studying the weapon in his hands. "Yes, sir. But there were no creatures like this—" he nodded at the alien bodies—"on Abydos. Those people were human . . . they were from earth. They were brought there by Ra thousands of years ago."

This was more than Samuels had heard O'Neill say at one time since they'd met. It was different, somehow, hearing the words out loud rather than just reading them in a dry report. He shivered. It was all ridiculous. Science fiction. Couldn't be real.

But there they were, lying dead and cold before him, and he had seen with his own eyes the devastation that innocent-looking staff had wrought.

Hammond snorted. "I know all about that. But your report said this *Ra* was in fact some kind of alien that lived inside a *human* body."

O'Neill's lip twitched. "Yeah, his eyes glowed. That was our first clue."

Definitely smart-ass. Samuels wondered fleetingly how the guy had ever made colonel.

Apparently so did the general. "Are you sure he's dead, Colonel?"

O'Neill shrugged, shutting the weapon down. Once more it appeared to be an elaborately decorated, if rather odd-shaped, hiking staff. "Unless he could survive a tactical nuclear warhead blowing up in his face, yeah, I'm positive. Why?"

Hammond jerked his head toward the bodies. "Colonel, these . . . people . . . or whatever they are . . . were guarding another man who retreated back through the Stargate. I got a good look at his eyes, Colonel. They glowed."

The general kept up easily with the younger man as they strode down the long concrete corridor.

"How do you feel about the Stargate mission after all this time, Colonel?" Hammond asked. He was fairly sure he knew the answer, or at least what the answer would have been ten minutes ago, before O'Neill had seen the bodies. All the bodies, the human ones included.

"How d'you mean?" O'Neill's voice was neutral.

"Well, it's been over a year. Has your perspective changed?" *It's been over ten minutes. How about your perspective now?*

As they came up to the corner, O'Neill started to answer, his words still carefully chosen. "Well, sir, I think that—"

The two broke step to allow another to escort two men into a room just down the hall. As they passed, O'Neill, his initial response forgotten, said, "Was that—?"

Hammond smiled to himself. *Gotcha.* "Kawalsky and Ferretti, yes. Served under your command on the first Stargate mission." As they came to his office door, he gestured offhandedly. "After you, Colonel." Samuels followed after, breathless.

O'Neill stalked through the office, ignoring the chair the general offered. His eyes shifted from one corner of the room to another, as if seeking a trap, and he headed directly to a large window overlooking the next room, a briefing room with a long boardroom table.

Kawalsky and Ferretti sat on one side of the table. Two officers stood on the other, going through files, jabbing their fingers at the papers and asking questions. Kawalsky and Ferretti looked distinctly uncomfortable, sending covert glances at the man watching on the other side of the window.

Hammond watched as O'Neill leaned against the window frame, assessing the tension he could see in shoulders and neck.

"Tell me about Daniel Jackson, Colonel," he suggested delicately.

O'Neill had something else on his mind. "Why are they questioning my men?"

Hammond felt a flicker of satisfaction. So O'Neill's sense of responsibility hadn't been exaggerated after all. "They're not your men anymore, Colonel. You retired," he reminded him. After a pause, he prodded, "Daniel Jackson."

O'Neill still didn't look around. "You read the report." The words were bitten off.

"Yes." *And* . . . ?

"It's all there."

"*Is* it?" Samuels challenged. It was his turn to play bad cop for the general. Besides, he really wanted to know.

The implication was clear; it brought O'Neill around to face him. But the window didn't transmit sound very well. There was no way to know what Kawalsky and Ferretti were saying.

"What's this all about, General?" O'Neill asked harshly.

"You didn't like Daniel Jackson, did you?" Hammond asked.

That wasn't what O'Neill was expecting. He shrugged. "Daniel was a scientist. He sneezed a lot. Basically, he was a . . . geek. Sir."

"So you didn't have a lot of time for him."

O'Neill took exception. "I didn't say that. He also saved my life and found the way home for me and my men. A little thing like that kinda makes a person grow on you."

Hammond ruffled some papers, never taking his eyes from the tall man in front of him. "According to the mission brief, your orders were to go through the Stargate, to detect any possible threat to Earth, and if found, to detonate a nuclear device and destroy the gate on the other side."

"But that's not what you did, is it?" Samuels leaped in again. The major was good at this, Hammond noted. He'd make a decent half of an interrogation team, maybe. Someday.

A shadow of defensiveness crossed O'Neill's dark eyes. "Not right away. Ra's forces overpowered my team and took the weapon before I could arm it."

One of the signs of a really good officer, Hammond had always felt, was how he was at lying to his superiors. O'Neill was prevaricating, and he was pretty bad at it. Hammond smiled, tigerish.

Samuels saw it too, and went for the kill. "But with Dr. Jackson's help, you eventually regained control? And did, in fact, detonate the weapon? Yes?"

O'Neill cast an almost desperate glance

through the window to his two men. His answer, however, was prompt and straightforward. "Yes."

Hammond took over. "So, to the best of your knowledge, Daniel Jackson and everyone else you knew on Abydos are *dead*. Is that correct?"

O'Neill hesitated, swallowed. His tongue touched his lower lip. Aha, Hammond thought. You've got a tell, boy. "That's . . . correct."

"Good," the general purred. "Then you won't mind if I authorize a go-ahead on our plan." Standing, he led O'Neill out of the office, down the corridor, and into an elevator.

O'Neill took one last agonized look through the window at his men and followed him.

"This quartz material the Stargates are made of," Hammond said musingly, never taking his eyes off O'Neill's, "it must be tough stuff if it can withstand a Mark 3."

"We sent a robot probe through after we got back, sir. It was flattened on the other end. Obviously the Abydos Stargate had been buried in the rubble." He was stalling. Hammond could tell that O'Neill could hear it in his voice as well as the general himself could.

"Well, somehow it got unburied," the general informed him.

They entered the Gate room.

The place was buzzing with activity. Hammond watched as O'Neill glanced around the room, at first registering only the signs of the damage resulting from the firefight, then focusing on the radio-controlled cart at the bottom of the ramp and the large, glistening metal cylinder it carried. Technicians swarmed around the device, making adjustments, reading ohmmeters, taking notes. A look of sheer horror crossed O'Neill's face.

"My God," he whispered. Then, louder, "You're sending another bomb?"

Hammond nodded almost jovially. "A Mark 5 this time. If these creatures did reopen the Abydos gate, we intend to reseal it for good." As he spoke, a digital timer on the cylinder's side lit up and started ticking off seconds.

"General, you can't do that!"

Hammond's eyes grew wide, smiling, innocently inquiring. "The countdown has already started. . . . Unless, of course, you have something to add?"

The general could almost hear the gears working in the other man's head. When O'Neill stepped forward to stand before him, for the first time the colonel stood at attention, ramrod straight, his eyes focused steadily on Hammond's.

"General Hammond, sir," he said, his voice staccato, emotionless. "I regret to inform you that my report was not entirely accurate."

"You didn't detonate the bomb." *Surprise, surprise.* He'd known there had to be something wrong in that report; aliens couldn't invade out of a Gate shattered to glowing radioactive rubble. And he'd known it had to have been O'Neill at the core of it. It had been his mission. His report.

His lie.

O'Neill's line of sight never wavered, but his tongue touched his lip again. *There's that tell again, boy. Tough, isn't it?* "No, I did detonate the bomb. It was aboard Ra's spacecraft.

It did kill him and eliminate the risk to earth."

"However?" Samuels said triumphantly.

"However," O'Neill admitted painfully, to Hammond, not Samuels, "Ra's ship was in orbit above the planet at the time, sir. Neither the gate nor anything else on the planet was destroyed. Daniel Jackson is alive and living with the people on Abydos."

And as a result four—probably five—good soldiers are dead. With an effort Hammond restrained his roar. "You violated direct orders? Why?"

"Because the people of Abydos are no threat to us. They deserve to be left alone."

"That's not up to you—" Hammond began.

O'Neill interrupted. "With all due respect, if I hadn't reported the Gate on the other side was destroyed, you would have sent another bomb. Just like you were *about* to. It wasn't necessary to let those people die; the threat from Ra was gone."

Apparently confession was good for the military soul as well; O'Neill had regained his mental balance and self-assurance.

Major Samuels wasn't ready to let go. "What

about that probe we sent through? It got crushed instantly."

O'Neill turned slightly to him, relaxing his ramrod posture. "After we went home, Jackson buried the Gate in rocks, making my return—or anyone else's—impossible."

· Hammond had heard the confession, but forgiveness was still up in the air. "Those four bodies lying in the morgue say otherwise." He turned to the technicians, who had paused in their scurrying to eavesdrop. "We'll send the bomb through on schedule."

"General, you can't do that!"

The boy had a pretty good roar himself. However, O'Neill was still a colonel—retired—addressing a general. "Oh, I can't?" Hammond said dangerously.

"There are innocent people on that planet," O'Neill protested.

"There are innocent people *here*," Hammond lashed back. He drew a deep breath, calming himself before continuing. "I have my orders too, Colonel. I *obey* mine." To the MPs standing behind Samuels, he said, "Take Colonel O'Neill to the holding room. Give him some time to think about things while I decide what to do with him."

The MPs stepped forward. O'Neill, ironic to the last, executed a textbook salute before turning on his heel to march off between them.

CHAPTER THREE

The MPs ushered him into his "cell," a small windowless room that had obviously been someone's office not too long before. It had been enhanced with a couple of bunks and a small table to go with the gunmetal gray desk.

Charles Kawalsky bolted to his feet, hand at his brow. "Colonel O'Neill, sir!"

O'Neill looked at him wearily, refusing to remember his own starched reaction not that long before. "I'm retired, Kawalsky. Lose the salute."

Kawalsky's hand drifted down, O'Neill grabbed it with both hands and shook it. *See? Civilian*, he told himself. *This is what civilians do, remember?*

Kawalsky sat, off balance mentally if not

physically. "Me and Ferretti didn't tell them anything," he said, trying to be reassuring.

It misfired, through no fault of his own; O'Neill was sure the room was bugged, that he'd been put in here with a member of his former command just so Hammond could hear what they had to say. But he'd told the truth now, all the truth that mattered, and he didn't care much what Hammond heard. He was trying to think of an argument to keep the general from sending that Mark 5 through the Gate. There were women and kids over there, innocent victims of Ra. They didn't deserve to die because of a paranoid general.

Though, he admitted to himself with a wrench, he could understand exactly where Hammond was coming from.

It didn't matter if he understood, approved, or even liked it, though. He'd had direct orders and had consciously chosen to disobey them. He'd never done that before in his whole career—in his whole life.

The fact that it was the right thing to do didn't mean he could avoid the consequences.

But it was *his* responsibility, *his* choice. There was no reason Kawalsky and Ferretti should have to suffer for it. He owed it to his men to make things right for them. "I appreciate that," he said.

"Hey," Kawalsky went on defiantly, "those kids on Abydos saved my life too."

"The kids. Yeah . . ." The kids. Especially the one kid who had wormed his way past all the defenses . . .

"I mean, they were the whole reason we kept the secret, right?" Kawalsky was still talking as if they were old comrades exchanging reminiscences at a bar somewhere. "That one kid idolized you. Remember him? Weird name, what was it . . . ?"

"Skaara." Skaara. Skaara, who could never take Charlie's place but had carved a place of his own in a mourning father's heart. The thought brought up a vivid image of a little, wool-clad Arab kid with long dark hair and bright eyes.

And that reminded him of another kid, with the same sharp eyes but blond hair instead, and he flinched.

Kawalski mocked up an awkward salute. "Remember how he was always saluting you?"

O'Neill forced a smile. "Yeah. My kid used

to do that when he was little." His voice stayed steady. He was proud of that. "Skaara kinda reminded me of him."

Kawalski blinked. "You an' me went through that whole mission together. I never even knew you had a son."

"He died just before the Abydos mission." O'Neill didn't want to continue the conversation. He didn't want to go on to the next memory, of a gleaming semiautomatic pistol lying on pale white carpet, a small empty hand lying nearby. And he refused the next image entirely.

"I'm sorry, sir, I had no idea."

O'Neill shook his head. He thought about saying more and decided not to. That wound wasn't healed. He didn't deserve to have it heal.

It had been a year since the two of them had seen each other, and Kawalsky was eager to talk about what he'd been doing, his promotion to major, even how he'd been summoned in the dead of night to return to the Stargate base. O'Neill listened, provided the proper noises to keep the man talking, and buried himself in his own thoughts.

Abydos. Better to think of Abydos, of Skaara, than Charlie. It still filled him with wonder, knowing he was one of the first modern men to walk on an alien planet. He'd been brought up on Heinlein, Clarke, Bradbury, Asimov, had stayed up all night to watch the Apollo landing. But as he grew older and the space program kept getting cut back, he'd abandoned his childhood dreams of being an astronaut and applied himself to more practical matters. He'd kept an eye on the Voyager and Explorer reports, shook his head over the Mir snafus, but never really thought seriously about going into space.

And then after Charlie died—he blinked at the stab of emotional pain—he'd never really thought seriously of anything at all.

And after all that, going into space turned out to be as easy as falling off a log. Or falling through a looking glass. And there was a wonderland with three moons waiting on the other side. A planet full of people from earth. People he couldn't bring himself to destroy.

After a while even Kawalski ran down. O'Neill couldn't find anything to talk about. The two men sat. Waited.

They were grateful for the sound of the twisting doorknob.

Hammond stood in the doorway, a pair of MPs at parade rest behind him. Kawalsky rocketed to attention. O'Neill got to his feet more slowly.

"How many people did you say are on Abydos?" the general asked. He looked as if he'd bitten into something awful but was determined to swallow it anyway.

Aha, thought O'Neill. *The old man had been listening after all.* "That we saw? Maybe five thousand." At least. But he wasn't going to shade his reporting any more.

The general came in and sat on one of the cots, facing his prisoners, waving Kawalsky to at ease.

"Does this mean you're reconsidering sending the bomb?" O'Neill asked. *Does this mean you're reconsidering blowing Skaara and Daniel Jackson to radioactive flinders?*

"It means I'm open to suggestions," Hammond replied heavily. He had the air of a man who'd spent a lot of time thinking, a lot of time on the phone with the powers that be.

"General, let me take a team through the

Gate. We'll find out who these aliens are." He waved at the other man. "Kawalsky and I have been there before. We know the lay of the land, and we know the people."

Hammond wanted to be convinced. He wanted it so much, O'Neill saw, that he had to resist the suggestion. "You *think* you know. Jackson could be dead. You don't know what you'd be walking into."

The memory of four dead enlisted personnel, the scarring on the walls in the Gate room, was clear in his eyes. O'Neill acknowledged it. If the Ra aliens were using the Abydos Gate again, there was no telling what had happened to the people on the other side. They might be prisoners. Dead. Vanished. On the other hand . . .

Maybe no. Maybe Skaara and Jackson were still there.

He could go back to the stars. And he didn't even have to be assigned to NASA first. "One way to find out."

Hammond sighed and nodded. Kawalsky, not nearly as enthusiastic about whatever wild idea O'Neill might have, merely looked at his former commander.

"Right," said Hammond. "We'll have the prototype probe shipped from MIT."

"No, no," O'Neill contradicted. "We don't need a probe."

"We don't?" Kawalsky said faintly.

O'Neill looked around the room, spotted what he was looking for on the gunmetal gray table. "This'll do." It was perfect. It was exactly what they needed.

It was a box of white Kleenex.

O'Neill led the charge out the door, catching Kawalsky flat-footed. Hammond followed, game but confused. The major lunged to catch up.

Minutes later, O'Neill, Kawalsky, Samuels, and Hammond stood in the control room overlooking the Stargate. Twenty soldiers in flak jackets, armed to the teeth, pointed rifles at the Gate below, their hands shifting uneasily on their weapons. Behind them, civilian technicians were hunched over their equipment. A computer screen over their heads showed symbols, shifting.

"Chevron four, encoded," one of the technicians announced.

Hammond was still looking at the Kleenex box. "Care to explain this concept?"

As they watched, the inner ring of the Stargate rotated, matching symbols with those in the outer ring. Above their heads the symbols on the screen shifted correspondingly, like a combination lock clicking into place. As each one slipped into place, a chevron-shaped frame on the gate glowed, and along the side of the computer screen another symbol was recorded.

"Chevron five, encoded."

The inner circle spun back almost 360 degrees.

"Jackson has allergies," O'Neill said absently, his full attention on the Gate. He still carried the box of tissues in his hand.

Behind him, Kawalski grinned. "I get it!"

Samuels didn't.

"Chevron six, encoded."

"He'll know it came from me and not, with all due respect, sir, from someone like you."

Hammond's brows knitted briefly.

Smiling, carrying his no–lotion, unscented, unmistakable message, O'Neill headed down from the control room to the Gate, leaving the others staring after him.

The room was vibrating. Shaking. The inner wheel rotated.

"Chevron seven, *encoded.*"

A fountain of blue light, quantum particles as disciplined as water, blasted into the room, reaching nearly to the bottom of the ramp where O'Neill stood. He was much calmer about it than anyone else watching.

The funnel snapped backward, through the back of the Gate, and then leveled off, shimmering.

A very self-possessed Jack O'Neill walked up the ramp and without hesitation poked the box of tissue through the wall of light. The Kleenex vanished.

Moments later, the Gate shut down. Silence descended on the room. Technicians and military men stared at each other.

O'Neill returned to the control room to see the computer image replaced by a star map. He watched with interest as a small X, indicating the probable path of the box of Kleenex, described a path along a probable wormhole between the Stargate on Earth and the one on Abydos.

The chief technician cleared his throat. "The,

um, the *object* should reach its destination in five seconds. Four. Three. Two. One.

"The object should now be through the Abydos Stargate." The words echoed in the room. They were all holding their breath.

"Now what?" Hammond demanded.

O'Neill grinned. "Now we wait. If Daniel's still around, he'll know what the message means."

"What if the aliens got it?" Samuels wasn't handling O'Neill's attitude at all well.

O'Neill pretended horror at the very concept. "Well, they could be blowing their noses right now!"

"They *could* be planning an attack," Samuels said stiffly.

O'Neill shook his head. "Oh, c'mon, Samuels, let me be the cynic around here." He gave the other man a look that carried the clear message, *I've been there. Have you?*

Then, looking back to Hammond, he added, "Sir, this could take some time."

It took a long time. The party had moved up to the observation deck-briefing room, most of them sitting around the table adding to a collection of empty coffee cups and imitation cream packets. At first they'd been tense, waiting for something to happen at any second—a full-fledged alien invasion perhaps—to come back out through the Gate. As the hours passed, the unbearable tension had diminished. Now there were signs that some of them wanted to call it quits and go to bed.

Jack O'Neill stood by the widow, almost exactly where he had stood before, one arm up along the frame, watching the Gate. He paced. He sprawled in a chair across the table from Hammond, chewing his thumbnail. Was that— They'd been there a long time; perhaps he was imagining—

Vibration.

It wasn't his imagination.

It was the Gate powering up. Hammond and Samuels moved to join him. Below them the guard squad was in readiness, rifles aimed at the empty hole that was the Gate.

Not one of them fired when the fountain of quantum particles shot out into the room. By the time O'Neill and Hammond made it down the spiral staircase from the observation desk, the shimmering surface of the open Gate was in place, and the room was eerily silent.

Then, abruptly, something spat out of the right surface. In a sterling example of military discipline, the squad held their fire; the Gate closed. Through it they could see the back of the room again.

It was as if nothing had happened at all.

Except that now, resting on the previously empty ramp, was a frosted-over Kleenex box. Empty.

O'Neill walked up the ramp and picked it up, turning it over in his hands. The rush of relief he felt made him dizzy for a moment: he was right. Daniel was there. And Skaara would be there too. They were still alive. They were all right. He couldn't prevent the smile that lighted up his face as he tossed it to the XO. Samuels looked it over carefully, then showed Hammond the patterned side of the box. Written in some kind of paint were the English words, *Thanks. Send more.*

Hammond snorted.

With exquisite military courtesy O'Neill asked, "Permission to take a team through the Stargate, sir?"

Hammond tried and failed to prevent a sigh of resignation, as if all this was still against his better judgment. "Assuming I get the President's authorization . . . The mission briefing will be at 0800 hours. Consider yourself recalled to active duty, Colonel."

CHAPTER FOUR

George Hammond had had a hard night. On one hand he was profoundly relieved not to be sending the Mark 5 through the Stargate: the idea of throwing a weapon that powerful at an invisible target, with no way to assess its effect, offended his sense of tactics. On the other hand, he couldn't shake the memory of those glowing eyes. He could stand up to nearly anything human, even Democrats, but meeting the gaze of something he *knew* to be alien would unnerve anyone.

On the third hand, not killing five thousand innocent civilians who had nothing to do with the aliens was always a good thing. Hammond had nothing against military necessity, but he hated waste on principle.

Which led him to another good thing: the return of the prodigal son—or perhaps black sheep—to the military fold. He looked up from his place at the observation deck table to see Colonel Jack O'Neill come in, exactly two minutes early, shaved, trim, back in uniform, sidearm and boots gleaming. He bore scarcely any resemblance to the scruffy leather-jacketed lumberjack of the day before. That was definitely a good thing; he'd been shamefully wasted in retirement.

O'Neill knew it too. He was barely able to restrain a smile as he returned the salute by the others in the room, rendered one himself to Hammond. Hammond was glad to return it. O'Neill was a military man, dammit, a good one. It was good to have him back.

Time to get this show on the road. Hammond looked around the table, accounting for everyone except—

"Where's Carter?" he asked Samuels.

"Just arriving, sir," the major replied. *And boy, am I glad I'm not the one who's late*, his expression said.

"Carter?" O'Neill asked, examining the file

in front of him. He had remained standing to conduct the briefing.

"I'm assigning Sam Carter to this mission," Hammond informed him.

"I prefer to choose my own team," O'Neill protested, seating himself.

Hammond could sympathize, but "Not on this mission. Sorry. Carter's our expert on the Stargate."

O'Neill wasn't happy about it. "Where's he transferring from?" *Give me some background on this guy*, he was asking. *Let me know if I can rely on this guy in a fight.*

From the doorway a feminine voice answered, *"She* is transferring from the Pentagon."

O'Neill swiveled his chair deliberately to look the newcomer over. Carter was starched and businesslike. But she was late. And she was a lowly captain.

And she was female. Blonde, short, fluffy hair, medium height, slender. Wearing brightly polished captain's bars on her painfully neat blue uniform. A very attractive female.

Hammond watched carefully as O'Neill got to his feet again and held out his hand to shake.

Carter declined the courtesy, instead standing to attention and saluting. O'Neill shifted gears without hesitation, returning the salute.

"Captain Samantha Carter, reporting, sir."

Back at the table, Major Kawalsky muttered, just loud enough to be heard, "But, of course, you go by 'Sam.'"

As the newcomer seated herself, she gave him an icy glance. "You don't have to worry, Major. I played with dolls as a kid." Hammond watched the interplay with silent interest. It was going to be up to O'Neill to weld this team into a fighting command. It was also going to be fun watching him do it.

"GI Joe?" Kawalsky wasn't going to let it go.

"Major Matt Mason." Carter wasn't backing down. She'd probably met this attitude many times before.

"Who?" Kawalsky asked, thrown off base by the unfamiliar answer.

"Major Matt Mason—Astronaut doll," Ferretti filled in. He went on to ask Carter, "Did you have that cool backpack that made him fly?"

Carter grinned at him, finding a kindred soul at last.

This was getting out of hand. While it was nice to see that Carter had something in common with at least one member of the team, this was a briefing, not a discussion of childhood toys.

"Let's get started," Hammond said. "Colonel?" *It's your team and your mission, mister. Time to take over.*

O'Neill picked up the cue and looked at Carter. "Right. For those of you on your first trip through the Gate"—*and that means you, lady, the rest of us have been there and done that already*—"you should be prepared for what to expect."

"I've practically memorized your report from the first mission," she said, answering the unasked question. "I like to think I've been preparing for this all my life."

Kawalsky grinned condescendingly. "Um, I think what the colonel is trying to say is . . ." He searched momentarily for a sufficiently intimidating example, "Have you ever pulled out of a simulated bombing run in an F-16 at eight-plus Gs?"

"Yes," she said matter-of-factly.

Kawalski picked up his dropped jaw and riposted feebly, "Well, it's way worse than that."

Ferretti nodded earnestly. "By the time you get to the other side you're frozen stiff, like you've just been through a blizzard naked."

"That's from the compression your molecules undergo during the millisecond required for reconstitution," she informed him.

A pained look crossed O'Neill's face. "Ah, here we go. Not another scientist, please?" he asked Hammond.

"Theoretical astrophysicist," Carter amended precisely.

O'Neill looked at her exasperatedly. "Which means what exactly?"

Hammond hid a grin. "Which means she is smarter than you are, Colonel." He waited a beat for O'Neill to be outraged, and added, "Especially in matters related to the Stargate."

Ferretti and Kawalsky chortled.

Carter nodded, oblivious to the breach in military discipline and good order the general had just handed O'Neill. "Colonel, I was studying Gate technology for two years before Daniel Jackson made it work and before you both went through. I should have gone through then." She leaned forward with the intensity of the point she was ramming home.

72

"Sir, you and your men might as well accept the fact that I *am* going through this time."

Air Force colonels were not accustomed to being addressed in this fashion by mere captains. "With all due respect, *Doctor*—" O'Neill began icily.

"In the military it's proper to refer to a person by their rank, not their title. You should call me Captain, not Doctor."

Hammond hastily forestalled O'Neill's eruption at being lectured on military etiquette by a mere junior officer. "Captain Carter's assignment to this unit is not an option. It's an order."

Still lecturing, Carter went on, "I'm an Air Force officer, just like you are, Colonel. And just because my reproductive organs are inside instead of outside doesn't mean I can't handle whatever you can handle."

O'Neill smiled gently, rather as a shark might on spotting a particularly appetizing swimmer. "Oh, this has nothing to do with you being a woman! I *like* women! It's *scientists* I have a problem with."

Carter clearly didn't believe him. "Colonel, I logged over a hundred hours in enemy airspace during the Gulf War. Is that tough enough for you? Or are we gonna have to arm wrestle?"

O'Neill opened his mouth, shut it again, and sat down. Whatever answer he might have made, he clearly thought better of.

Samuels cleared his throat. "I don't want to throw a damper on your enthusiasm, but I still say the safest, most logical thing to do is bury the Gate just as the ancient Egyptians did—make it impossible for the aliens to return. It's the only way to eliminate the threat."

O'Neill gave Samuels a look that said, you're a desk jockey, right? And I can *deal* with *you.* "Except it won't work."

"It worked before," Hammond offered, playing devil's advocate.

O'Neill shook his head. "They know what we are now, how far we've come. We're a threat to them." He indicated the Stargate in the room below. "How do you think this thing got to Earth in the first place?"

"Good question," Hammond said, when no one else seemed inclined to answer.

"They've got *ships*, General. Ra had one as big as the great pyramids. They don't *need* the

Stargate to get here; they can do it the old-fashioned way. With all due respect to Mr. Glass-Is-Half-Empty over here, don't you think maybe we should use the Stargate to do some recon before they decide to come back? Again?"

Hammond thought about it. O'Neill was right, of course. Burying the Gate would deny access to the aliens temporarily perhaps, but it would also deny the stars to a human race who had a long way to go before they had ships of their own.

Still, the only thing they knew for sure was on the other side of that Gate was an alien with glowing eyes. Who might or might not use Kleenex.

"I'll give you exactly twenty-four hours to either return or send a message through," he decided. "A real one, no Kleenex boxes. Otherwise, we assume the worst and send the bomb through."

O'Neill's response was prompt. "Understood."

He'd fudged on his orders last time, Hammond thought. Or maybe he'd just been displaying appropriate initiative for the senior

officer in the field, commanding. Who knew?
Still, he found himself liking the man, understanding his reasons even if he didn't approve.
Protecting the innocent was a duty all too
many military personnel ignored.

He'd feel a whole lot more confident about
the future of this team, though, if he hadn't
seen the glance O'Neill and Carter exchanged.
Those two weren't finished.

Hammond was still thinking about it a few
hours later, when the fully equipped team, kit-
ted out in desert fatigues, lined up at the base
of the ramp to exchange a farewell salute.
O'Neill, Carter, Ferretti, Kawalsky, a couple of
others—it bothered the general that he didn't
know their names. He ought to know the
names of the people he was sending so un-
imaginably far, into such danger.

"Try to follow orders this time, Colonel," he
said softly to O'Neill.

O'Neill looked innocent. "Sir?"

Hammond looked him in the eye. "This time
you bring Daniel Jackson back. Is that clear?"

O'Neill didn't blink. "Yes, sir."

With a roar the Gate activated. Hammond

and Samuels moved out of the way, and O'Neill turned to Carter, who was staring at the whiplashing surge of quantum particles with wide eyes. "Captain?"

Still defensive, she snapped, "Don't worry, Colonel. I won't let you down."

O'Neill sighed. "Good. I was going to say, 'Ladies first.' "

Slightly abashed, she muttered, "You really will like me when you get to know me."

"Oh, I adore you already, Captain," O'Neill said, clearly doubting it.

The two nameless soldiers marched up the ramp and into the gate. The pool reached out to swallow them up.

Kawalsky and Ferretti followed, marching steadfastly through with their eyes closed tight.

Carter walked up more slowly, holding her breath, and touched the surface gingerly with one forefinger, then her whole arm. A delighted smile crossed her face. "The energy the Gate must release to form a stable wormhole— it's astronomical, to use exactly the right word!"

O'Neill looked back at Hammond, grimacing. Daniel Jackson had reacted exactly this way when he'd first gone through the Stargate too, more than a year ago. *Scientists*, the look of disgust said, and with that he pushed her into the shimmering pool and through the Gate. A moment later, he squared his shoulders and followed her.

Samantha Carter had memorized the reports, all right. Unfortunately, she'd forgotten that a good military report removes all personality. O'Neill's remarks on the passage through the Stargate had read:

Passage through the Gate proved to be unsettling and detrimental to combat readiness. This effect lasted only a short time, however, and knowledge of what to expect made the return to Earth much easier.

That didn't adequately describe the light, the stars, the sensation of weightless spinning in a vortex of color, flipping up and down and end over end like a sparrow caught in a force ten hurricane, so cold she felt that her guts would shatter, so dizzy—

The first thing she did as she stumbled out of the Gate was fall to her knees and throw up.

Behind her, she was dimly aware of Jack

O'Neill, covered with frost, looking at her with contempt.

"Oh, maybe you shouldn't have had that big lunch," he commiserated. He was already on his feet, checking the place out.

The words made her angry enough to quell the nausea and stop retching. Wiping the back of her hand over her mouth, she looked around at the rest of the team.

They were in a great stone room, its ceiling supported by a series of columns. This must be the Gate room on Abydos; she recognized the Egyptian-looking hieroglyphics that covered the walls. Figures half-human, half-animal, sun figures, feathers, chariots, here and there a creature that had never been seen on Earth, all in the two-dimensional style of the New Kingdom back home. The colors here, though, were bright and new, red and blue and yellow and green and black, with here and there a hint of gold leaf. She staggered to her feet, nausea forgotten, and stumbled closer, straining in the dim light to see these artifacts of an alien planet. Around her the others were also on their feet, checking over their supplies and weapons.

Suddenly it wasn't such an effort to see anymore. Carter blinked at the abrupt brightness and turned.

She blinked again, trying to focus against the glare of more than a dozen torches. It was no use. No matter how hard she squeezed her eyes shut, when she opened them again she still saw a ragged skirmish line of children, boys, wearing rags . . . and aiming very familiar Earth-style, Air Force-issue M-16s at them.

CHAPTER FIVE

Outside, the wind howled. Sand, flung against stone, sounded like radio static. From reading the report, Carter had the distinct impression that the inhabitants of Abydos—descendants apparently of Egyptian *fellahin*, or tribesmen from at least five thousand years ago—had never reached a level of technology that would allow the invention of radio.

Perhaps weapons were easier to invent.

She got to her feet very slowly, terribly conscious of the dozens of dark eyes staring at her over the muzzles of the rifles. The rest of the team stood as if waiting for something to break the impasse.

"Cha'hali. Cha'hali—lower your guns."

Carter didn't know what startled her more—

hearing the very American accent or the translation of the phrase.

The young men lowered their weapons almost reluctantly, and glancing over their shoulders, they made way for the newcomers. Carter looked to the colonel for direction. He, Kawalsky, and Ferretti were smiling, a light of welcome in their eyes.

"Hello, Jack. Uh—" The speaker glanced at the still threatening weapons. "Welcome back."

It was—it had to be—Daniel Jackson, Carter realized. The archaeologist, a man not that much older than the youngsters around him, was slight and fair, his blond hair in contrast to their darker hues. He still wore some Earth clothing, but supplemented now with rough cloth where it had worn out. Light glinted off round, wire-rimmed spectacles. His nose was a bit red, as if he had a cold.

She had spent hours poring over this man's work, trying to apply principles of physics to ancient human history. Seeing him standing there in the flesh was a bit unnerving. He looked smaller than his reports.

O'Neill, however, wasn't looking at Jackson. He was looking past him, at an older boy (or perhaps a young man), one of the ones holding guns on the team. Clad in heavy, rough-woven cloth, the boy showed his Middle Eastern Earth ancestry in sharp black eyes and slender, tough build. His hair was a mass of coarse black braids. He held the weapon as if he knew exactly what to do with it.

"Skaara?" The word was full of gladness, with the slightest edge of uncertainty: a do-you-remember-me greeting. It was interesting seeing O'Neill show uncertainty, a new, perhaps more vulnerable side to him than she had seen before.

As Carter watched, the boy smiled back, white teeth gleaming. Then he shoved his weapon into the hands of someone next to him, and gave O'Neill a passable salute. Uncertainty gone, O'Neill crisply returned the gesture and moved past Jackson to embrace Skaara in a bear hug.

"I did not think I am seeing you again," the boy said when he could get his breath.

O'Neill stood back from him, looking him up and down as if at a long-missed child at a family reunion. Carter could almost hear his "Look how much you've grown!" He was grinning, delighted. Kawalsky and Ferretti were grinning too.

Jackson cleared his throat gently. O'Neill, brought back from whatever memories he was comparing to the present, looked up, recognized him, and went to shake his hand. "How are you, Daniel?"

"Good," Jackson said simply. "You?"

It was as if nothing special had happened, two friends who had been apart for a while running into each other in downtown Abydos. Carter shook her head. At least in greeting Skaara, O'Neill had demonstrated something beyond his usual sardonic self-possession. Now he was firmly back in character. It must be a guy thing, she thought cynically.

"Better," he said, "now that I see you guys are okay."

Kawalsky and Ferretti joined the reunion. Carter and the other two soldiers, feeling more than a bit left out, shuffled uneasily as they shook hands and slapped shoulders.

"Greetings from Earth, Dr. Jackson," Ferretti said.

Jackson smiled. "Hello, Ferretti—Kawalsky." He turned to draw a woman forward out of the shadow of the pillar she had been hiding behind. "Sha're? Don't be shy."

Sha're took Jackson's hand and ventured out, blushing. She was a beautiful woman, with long blue-black hair and a distinct family resemblance to Skaara. Jackson's attitude toward her was protective, gentle as he slipped an arm around her. Despite herself, Carter felt a quickly quashed flash of envy.

O'Neill, exercising the gentleman part of the officer-and mandate again, took Sha're's hand. "It's good to see you again." She smiled and blushed even more, and the colonel leaned over and kissed her cheek.

Not military, Carter thought indignantly. Not military at all. She turned away from the reunion and began examining a stone panel set next to the Abydos gate. Someone had to keep their mind on duty, after all. . . . The panel was a double ring of the Stargate symbols, encircling a large dome of translucent, roughly polished material that looked like fractured rose quartz.

"So. I knew it was only a matter of time before you had to tell the truth about us still being here," Jackson was saying.

O'Neill shrugged in acknowledgment. "Why the militia? Has something else come through?"

Jackson adjusted his glasses. "No. Just taking precautions. Why?"

Half listening, Carter traced the symbols on the small panel. With a jolt she realized what it was. "*This* is how they controlled it! It took us fifteen years and three supercomputers to MacGyver a control system for the gate on Earth!"

Somewhere through her shock she could hear O'Neill's mildly exasperated "Captain . . ."

"Look how *small* it is!"

"Captain!"

This time she heard him. The whip crack of his voice brought her around to see the rest of them staring at her.

Recovering herself, she stepped forward to offer Jackson her hand, carefully avoiding looking at her commanding officer. "Dr. Jackson, I presume. I'm Dr. Samantha Carter."

"I thought you wanted to be called 'Captain,'" O'Neill observed. Carter didn't bother to dignify that with a reply. Jackson glanced at the colonel but seemed to take his snideness for granted.

The archaeologist finally exerted some control over the conversation. "What's going on, Jack?"

O'Neill turned back to him. "We're here because six hostile aliens came through the Stargate on Earth. Four people are dead; one's missing."

"One of them looked like Ra, Daniel," Kawalsky added.

The surrounding natives, particularly Skaara and Sha're, understood enough of what was being said to know that there was trouble. The mention of Ra confirmed it. The room buzzed, and several of the boys shifted their grip on their weapons.

Jackson polished his glasses, a gesture that looked more like a nervous habit than a necessary one. "Well, they didn't come from *here*. The boys take shifts guarding it thirty-six hours a day, every day. We'd know if they came through here."

O'Neill let out a long breath. "Well, they came from somewhere, Daniel. I'm gonna have to look around."

Jackson nodded. "I think I can help you find out who it was, but it's going to have to wait until the sandstorm is over." Then, as if remembering his manners, "We were about to have our evening meal. Why don't you join us?"

The room next to the Abydos Gate room had all the signs of being inhabited by a scholar, with stacks of notes on material that looked much like papyrus. It was a living and cooking area too. A mouthwatering smell rose from the metal dish on the fire as Sha're stirred.

The dish, Carter noted, didn't fit in with the apparent technology of the people of Abydos. It was dented but too shiny.

Apparently O'Neill noticed it too. "I'm sure the people at MIT will be happy to know their million-dollar probe also makes very good cookware."

Daniel looked a trifle embarrassed. "Well, um, it got pretty banged up when it came through the gate into our barricade so we . . . made use." He looked at Sha're, who laughed and fed him a piece of meat. "And it *is* non-stick titanium, so . . ." He smiled at Sha're in return. "Very good. Perfect. *Beanaa wa.*" To the rest he added, "Everybody try this."

Carter followed instructions. The only part of the dish she could identify for sure was rice; the meat tasted, of course, like chicken. The vegetables were surprisingly crisp and tasty for having been boiled for who knew how long.

"This too," Skaara piped up, filling a canoe-shaped drinking vessel from a leather bag. He offered it to O'Neill, who was seated in place of honor near the fire.

"What is this?"

"Drink!" the boy said, eyes dancing.

O'Neill sniffed at the cup. "*Moonshine?* Skaara, did you make this?"

"Moon. Shine?" Skaara tried out the new word, looking down speculatively at his creation.

"As in booze. As in you're not old enough to *drink*. Give me that, for crying out loud. Daniel, what're you teaching these kids?"

Sha're laughed again and snuggled next to Daniel, who smiled too, ducking his head and surreptitiously reached for Sha're's hand. O'Neill took the cup from Skaara.

"Our little soldiers are growing up, Colonel," Kawalsky said.

"Yeah, I'm so proud." O'Neill looked extremely doubtful. Carter was glad that he was the one who had been selected to try whatever it was. She wasn't sure she could handle it.

She was part of the feast as a member of the team, and therefore also an honored guest—perhaps not quite as honored as O'Neill—but she could see the women chattering excitedly behind their hands about her. Sha're, sitting beside Daniel, was spending more time feeding him than eating herself. Carter wondered if the women usually ate separately from the men here. Very possible, considering their cultural origins, but none of her business, she reminded herself.

"You try!" Skaara urged.

O'Neill shook his head. "Okay, but too much of this is bad for you, you know that."

"He knows." Daniel's remark was almost as dry as O'Neill's.

O'Neill sipped and gasped as the drink hit his throat. "Oh, *aggghhh*. It's pure alcohol!"

"Moon. Shine."

"That's great, Skaara. Really." O'Neill caught

his breath. His face flushed red. "I . . . couldn't be more proud."

Grinning hugely, Skaara reached into a pouch on his belt, producing a cigarette lighter. He presented it to O'Neill with an air of someone finally surrendering a sacred trust.

The colonel blinked at the offering, startled, then shook his head. "I quit smoking. Besides, I told you to keep it."

Skaara tilted his head with an are-you-*sure*? gesture. When O'Neill nodded emphatically, the boy ran away, clutching the lighter.

"You know he's never had that out of his sight the whole time you were gone," Daniel remarked.

"*Really*?"

O'Neill might pretend otherwise, Carter thought, but she could tell that the colonel was touched. It was amazing, really: Daniel spoke of "the time you were gone" as if it was nothing more than a temporary interruption in O'Neill's relationship with this place and these people. The colonel, and Kawalsky and Ferretti too, had history with these people, she realized. They really mattered to the officers. It helped explain why O'Neill had . . .

misstated . . . matters in his report. She wasn't sure she could have blown them all up either.

A different side of the colonel indeed. She found herself eyeing him speculatively, wondering what other surprises that facade concealed.

"So, this man who looked like Ra," Daniel went on matter-of-factly, "he must've come through another Gate."

That jerked her out of her musing. "As in Stargate?" O'Neill asked, as startled as she was.

"What other Gates?" she demanded. "The Stargate only goes *here*."

Daniel waved his hand in a gesture—just a second, let me swallow this—and then said, "Well, um, I think you're wrong about that."

Carter was outraged. Who did this dirty, scruffy archaeologist-gone-native think he *was*? "I was *there*. We ran hundreds of permutations!"

Daniel nodded: Yes, yes, of course you did, I'm not saying you didn't work very hard. "But you didn't have what you need."

"What are you talking about, Daniel?" Despite the familiar address, the military edge was back in O'Neill's voice.

Before Jackson could answer, Skaara stuck his head back in the door. "Daniel, the storm is passed."

The archaeologist nodded. "I'll show you." He bounced to his feet. Sha're immediately rose to stand beside him. "Sha're, *ben qua ri,* Jack, and his friends . . . to see the *vili tao an.*"

The mixture of English and Abydos dialect seemed to work fine for communication. Sha're, however, was clearly upset. She gave all the team members, including Carter, an unhappy glare.

"*Bonni wai?*" It seemed she wanted to come along.

"We won't be gone long," he soothed her. Leaning over, he tried to give her a little kiss on the forehead. Sha're was having none of it; she embraced him, giving him an all-out, passionate kiss. The audience roared and cheered.

Sha're finally broke away. "Good-bye, my Daniel."

Jackson, stunned and possibly short of oxygen, stood there, staring at her. Finally he shook himself free of his testosterone-induced coma and forced himself to step away. If that wasn't a promise to come home to, Carter thought, nothing ever was.

Jackson, still blushing a fiery red, backed away from his wife and out the door, clearly almost as unwilling to leave her as she was to let him go.

They came out of the great pyramid of Abydos into the sunlight, whose glare reflected off the pale sand. "Can't say I missed this place," Kawalsky groused, squinting. Ferretti and the other two had remained behind in the shade and coolness of the pyramid room to set up their equipment.

"Come on," Jackson said, leading them down a steeply inclined ramp at least one hundred feet long, out of the building and onto Abydos proper.

Samantha Carter stopped two or three times as she went, the first time to look up at the three moons hanging huge in the daylight sky, then at the sheer size of the pyramid. It had to be at least ten times the size of Cheops's monument on Earth. The storm had drifted pale lemon-colored sand over the long ramp, but the pair of obelisks that marked the end, or the beginning, of the walkway still pierced at least eighty feet of sky.

"This is just incredible!" she breathed.

Daniel gave her a deprecating smile. "Oh, you ain't seen nothing yet."

Flying an F-16 over Iraq had not given Samantha Carter a real appreciation for what it was like to take a little walk in the desert. She slipped and slid up and down sand dunes, ignoring the glances O'Neill and Kawalsky gave her and the aborted effort to give her a hand up when she landed on her tailbone at the bottom of one particularly steep slope.

They circled around the little town—wherever they were headed, it wasn't there. The place looked too small to hold five thousand people, but since she never got inside, it was hard to tell. She could see a mud wall and some roofs but not much else. There must be a spring there; the food they'd eaten had to be grown somewhere, and Abydos didn't look like it supported much mass transport. Off in the distance she caught a glimpse of something that looked a lot like a woolly mammoth as imagined by Steven Spielberg, but there were

no roads. Just sand and, eventually, hills, covered with large boulders and small grayish
shrubs.

It was certainly easier to walk on rock than
sand. Looking back at their path, Carter was
surprised to still be able to see the pyramid
that marked the location of the Abydos Gate.
She'd thought they'd come much farther than
that.

"C'mon, Captain," O'Neill said. The men
were waiting for her up ahead. Any chinks in
that ironic armor had closed right up again.

A few steps more took them into a fissure in
the rock; the fissure led to a cave. The darkness—and drop in temperature—was a shock
compared to the blinding sunlight outside.

"I decided there had to be more to this place,
so I started exploring," Jackson explained, almost as if apologizing. "Just the area around
the town and the pyramid at first. After about
a month I found this place. Captain Doctor,
you're going to love this."

One by one, the boys who came along as
Daniel's honor guard and escort lit their
torches. O'Neill and Kawalsky, taking a more
practical approach, used flashlights.

They were needed. Even though the place already contained two tables, each bearing a circle of nine blazing torches with a tenth in the middle, they were needed.

The cave was immense. The roof peaked far over their heads. The walls were lined with carved black marble obelisks. Against one wall were a pair of enthroned statues of Egyptian gods, thirty feet tall. The statues faced a giant emblem carved into the opposite wall. The channel of the engraving had been filled with molten gold, creating an *iret wadjet*, otherwise called an eye of Horus.

But even more amazing than the *wadjet*-eye were the lines upon lines of carvings that occupied the walls of the room, floor to ceiling, between the obelisks. The towering stones too were covered with symbols. Unlike the eye of Horus, the symbols covering the rest of the room were not Egyptian, but combinations, variations, and permutations of the symbols on the Stargates.

"My God," Carter breathed. "This is amazing. This is the archeological find of the century." Or of the millennium. Or of the ages. She unlimbered her flashlight, shining it across the engravings, the carving on the obelisks. "Have you been able to translate it?" So eager to capture the images she was almost fumbling, she put down the flashlight for a camera and started taking photos.

"I think so," Jackson said diffidently.

"What's it say?" O'Neill wanted a practical answer.

"It doesn't say anything, really. Actually, it's sort of a chart, more of a map."

"Of?"

"Well, I haven't been able to analyze *all* of it. I mean, look at it. It would take my whole life." He sounded absolutely delighted at the prospect. An archaeologist's version of job security, Carter supposed, and without the irritation of writing a grant proposal either. She sympathized wholeheartedly.

The flash wasn't working well enough, and she broke out her video camera.

"Daniel"—O'Neill's exasperation was clear—"we don't have that much time. What's it a map of?"

Jackson nodded, stepping back to point at the rock as if he were in a lecture hall pointing at a very large overhead projection. "Well, the symbols seem to be separated clearly into groupings. Each grouping is attached to others with a line. And each grouping of glyphs contains seven symbols." He passed a hand through his hair, searching for simple words. "So you can see where this is going, of course."

"Tell us anyway," O'Neill said with a hard-held patience.

"All the symbols are on the Stargate in the Abydos chamber. I've also been able to chart some of them in the Abydos night sky. Or at least pretty close . . ."

This was not the clear, concise explanation O'Neill was waiting for. Daniel Jackson shook his head, unable to believe his friend couldn't see what was, to him at least, glaringly obvious.

"Jack, I think it's a map of a vast network of Stargates. Stargates that are all over the galaxy!"

Carter looked up from her camera. "I don't think that can be, Doctor."

"Why not?"

Carter could feel herself arming for an academic battle, may the best citations win.

"Because after Colonel O'Neill and his team

came back," she explained, "*my* team tried hundreds of symbol permutations, using Earth as the point of origin, and it never worked."

Daniel nodded eagerly. "I tried the same here, but it didn't work either. I figured the destinations I tried are destroyed or buried. But some of them somewhere *must* still exist."

Carter shook her head. "I don't think so."

Daniel, undefeated, leaned forward. "Then where did your Ra look-alike come from?" He appealed to O'Neill as adjudicator. "Look, I don't pretend to know anything about astrophysics, but couldn't the planets change? I mean, drift apart or something like that, to throw this map off?"

It was good. Really, really good. It was a pleasure to lose a session like this one, because in losing you gained a new perspective, and therefore you won no matter what. Carter's slightly patronizing smile vanished, replaced with one of appreciation. "I *knew* I'd like you."

Jackson looked back at her, mildly befuddled. "Really? I mean . . . You think I'm right?"

"According to the expanding universe model, all bodies in the universe are constantly moving farther apart."

"So in the thousands of years since the Stargate was built . . ."

She nodded. "All the coordinates could have changed."

Daniel's brows knitted as he proceeded to challenge his own theory. "But why does it still work between Abydos and Earth?"

"Abydos is probably the closest planet in the network to Earth. The closer they are, the less the difference in relative position due to expansion. The farther away, the greater the difference. In a few thousand years more, it won't work between Earth and Abydos either."

"Unless you can adjust to the displacement?"

O'Neill and Kawalsky swiveled their heads back and forth as if following a ball at a tennis match.

"With this map as a base," Carter said triumphantly, "that should be easy. All we have to do is correct for Doppler effect. Then I should be able to arrive at a computer model that will predict the adjustments necessary to get the Gate working again."

"So," Kawalsky interrupted, recognizing a capping argument when he heard one even if

he didn't understand it, "what'd we just figure out?"

Carter recognized it too, but she also saw
the ramifications. "Any civilization advanced
enough to build this Gate network would be
able to compensate for fifty thousand years of
stellar drift."

O'Neill was still slightly behind the curve.
"The Stargate can go other places?"

"The aliens could have come from . . .
anywhere."

O'Neill looked up at the carvings on the
wall, mentally calculating the number of possibilities the symbol groupings represented.
Thousands . . . thousands of new worlds . . .

"Sir, with your permission," Carter said
briskly, back in military mode, "I'd like to put
this entire room on digital video. Then when
we get back to Earth I can download it into
the computer and get faster results."

Shaken, O'Neill nodded. Thousands of new
worlds. How many of them occupied by aliens
with glowing eyes? "Do it. But do it quickly."

Louis Ferretti was working away at a laptop,
roughing out a report. He found himself dis-

tracted by Sha're and another Abydos woman, who were directing the teen militia in carrying in more food. The other two soldiers made no pretense of working; they were too busy enjoying the scenery. This was going to be a major feast, held in the Gate room itself, and the women were fussing like grandmothers at Thanksgiving dinner, making sure everything was perfect for their guests. The fact that they were already stuffed to the gills was a mere detail.

"You gotta give Daniel credit," Ferretti remarked idly, shutting the laptop down. "She is one beautiful woman."

Sha're, hearing the name of her beloved, looked up and smiled shyly.

Ferretti smiled back, wishing he'd gotten so lucky. He was thinking that some people had all the luck, being abandoned on another world and finding a beautiful woman who obviously adored them, when the room trembled with an ominously familiar vibration.

Sha're and the other woman looked up in terror. The boys and the three soldiers from Earth grabbed guns, scrambling, dishes of unidentifiable delicacies flying everywhere.

Ferretti dived for cover behind a stone bench as the Abydos Gate activated, spewing forth a funnel of quantum particles. Sure enough, as soon as the Gate stabilized, six Serpent guards came trooping out, followed by what looked very much like the same guy who'd come through the Earth Gate.

"*Damn* it!" Ferretti whispered, trying to get a good target.

The golden leader, seeing resistance, snapped to his guards, "*Brichnk!*"

The Serpent Guards opened fire with their odd-looking staff weapons. The stone benches behind which the boys and the soldiers were crouching disintegrated with a deafening roar, shards of stone flying like hail. The women screamed. Ferretti felt like screaming too, but he was too busy. He and the others returned fire, but the Serpent Guards' armor seemed impervious to mere high-velocity bullets. Ferretti kept firing as his two men jerked and fell, gaping holes blasted in their bodies; he kept firing as the boys shrieked and died, as Skaara dived behind a supporting pillar, motioning to Sha're to join him. The captain could barely hear the boy's call, "Sha're! *Shim rota! Shim rota!*"

Out of nowhere, a massive invisible hand struck Ferretti on the shoulder, spinning him back, knocking his rifle out of his hands. Dazed, he watched as the golden one caught sight of the frantic Sha're and yelled an order to his guards. Another blow slapped him across the face, and his left eye blurred.

One of the Serpent Guards responded instantly, grabbing the woman and dragging her to his leader. Skaara shrieked in rage and protest, lunging toward the aliens, firing wildly. Another guard lifted his staff weapon, and the long, narrow bulb on the end gaped wide, charging with evil energy. He pointed it toward the frantic boy, ready to destroy him, when another guard, evidently the commander, grasped the weapon and turned to the golden one.

"Chel Kol, Makka sha?"

Ferretti shook his head. His vision was blurring, but he could hear the words clearly. His shoulder—there was something about his shoulder he should notice—

He could hear the head guard talking to Skaara. "This is not your weapon. Where did you get it?"

The leader either didn't hear or wasn't interested in the answer. He was only a few feet from Ferretti as he smiled, baring his teeth, and reached forward to grab Skaara by the throat, lifting the boy into the air until he was eye to eye with the alien. Skaara's rifle clattered to the floor as the mask on the golden one's head folded back into itself, revealing a face that would be all too human were it not for the glowing eyes.

"A good choice, Teal'c," he said. "A perfect specimen."

English? Ferretti wondered. He was sagging back against the stone floor, watching as best he could through one half-closed eye. Well, why not English? Who knew what aliens could do?

A ribbon around the alien's hand and fingers began to glow as well, weaving a net of energy around the boy, through his neck and down his spine. Skaara fell limp, and the alien shoved his unconscious body into the arms of another of his guards.

The room echoed now. For a long moment, as the leader of the invading aliens surveyed the devastation he had wrought, the only sound was the crying of the women and the surviving children. At least six of the boys were dead, Ferretti thought hazily. The bastard looked proud of himself.

And then he turned to Sha're, pulling her to him, eyeing her like a prize racehorse. He pinched her cheeks, forced her mouth open to inspect her teeth, felt her hair. The woman was petrified but refused to collapse. The alien smiled, recognizing defiance, savoring it, and reaching out, he ripped her robe in half.

Gloating over her naked body, he smiled. "You may be the *one*."

Sha're pulled away, but was caught by the Serpent Guards. Ignoring her now, the leader strode to the ancient control panel, pushing buttons. Ferretti strained to see, to remember.

The Gate reactivated. Grabbing the woman by one arm, he pulled her through the portal.

His shoulder. His eye. They were beginning to demand attention all their own, Ferretti realized. It was no longer just a feeling of overwhelming pressure; it was real, right-now, agonizing *pain*.

As the Serpent Guards followed their leader

through the Gate, carrying Skaara and Sha're with them, his one good eye sagged shut, and he let blackness descend, shutting out the soft weeping of the children.

CHAPTER SIX

"Sha're!"

It was the first word out of Jackson's mouth. Even in the cave, they had felt the characteristic vibration that meant the Gate was powering up. They knew instantly that whoever was coming through didn't work for General Hammond, and they ran for the pyramid.

Jackson, O'Neill, Kawalsky, and Carter led the charge into the Gate room to find a scene of utter devastation. Some of the women were weeping over the bodies of the boys. Jackson ran to them, kneeling by the side of one of the stricken youths. Meanwhile, Carter and Kawalsky ran to the aid of their comrades, only to find that two of them were beyond their help. O'Neill took a quick survey of the room, making sure no hostiles remained and assessing overall damage. His lips were white with rage.

Samantha Carter checked Ferretti's pulse, gritting her teeth against the urge to retch at the sight and smell of the man's arm and the blood that covered his face and eye. She was relieved to find a sign of a heartbeat, thready and quick. Beside her Kawalsky broke out a medical kit and began cutting away the blood-soaked uniform.

Beneath their hands, Ferretti stirred and groaned. Carter moved to hush him, but Kawalsky held his hand up, retraining her.

"I . . . saw . . . the symbols . . ." They were rewarded with those few words before Ferretti fell back, mercifully unconscious.

Carter got to her feet. "Colonel! Ferretti saw the seven symbols."

Daniel, leaning over the boy, took him by the shoulders. "It's all right," he said. "Tell me what happened."

The boy shook his head. "It was Ra."

O'Neill's head snapped around. "What's going on, Daniel?"

Daniel was shaking his head, trying to understand as he talked to the boy. "Ra's dead. *Tao qua*, Ra."

"No, no, Ra. I saw! His eyes . . . He took Sha're. He took Skaara into the *Chaapa-ai*!"

Daniel went white. So did O'Neill.

"Where?" the archaeologist demanded. "Did you see?" Surrendering support of the boy to the surrounding women, he ran to the Gate control panel and pointed at the symbols. "Show me which pictures. Did you see?"

The boy shook his head, muttering, and then gasped once and sagged back, dead.

Kawalsky, finished with the rough bandaging of his friend's arm, looked up. "What's going on, Daniel? Could there be another Ra?"

The repetition of the question, the shock of the situation, caused something in Daniel Jackson to snap. "How the hell should I know? I should have left the barricade up. This is my fault. . . ."

Quietly, Carter asked for O'Neill's notice. "Colonel, Ferretti needs medical attention."

Jackson waved his arms distractedly. "Go. Help him. I can send you back—"

O'Neill shook his head. "You're coming with us this time, Daniel. I've got orders."

Jackson wheeled on him. "I don't care about your orders, Colonel. My *wife* is out there. So is *Skaara*—"

"And the only way you're going to get them back is to come home with us," O'Neill snapped. "Ferretti might've seen the coordinates for where they went."

Carter held up her digital video. "I've got all I need."

For a long moment Daniel Jackson stood lost, looking around at the people of Abydos. The room was crowded now with men and women from the town, parents of the boys who had fought in vain. They looked back at him, their stranger, their leader who had slain the monster Ra. What would he do now that Ra had come back, taking his revenge, taking Sha're and Skaara for his own evil purposes?

With Sha're gone, Jackson had lost the greatest link he had to Abydos. With Sha're gone, would he abandon them? Did he have any reason to stay? The happiness he had known had vanished, and in its place had reappeared the threat he thought was gone forever.

He took a deep breath and gathered them around himself. "After we go through the

Chaapa-ai," he said, "you have to bury it like we did before. Then leave this place."

"You come back?" asked one wistful voice from the back of the crowd.

He shook his head violently. "No. No, I can't, nobody can. That's what I'm telling you, not for a long time." He looked at the Gate with something close to hatred in his eyes. "Soon as we're gone, I want you to close it. Bury it, put a big, heavy cover stone over it. Nothing *good* can ever come through the Gate. Do you understand?"

The voice refused to accept this. "*You* came through it, Dani-el." The owner of the voice, one of the young boys, broke free of the group and stood in front of him, defiant.

Daniel's hand touched the dark head, a gesture oddly like that of an Old Testament patriarch, and his voice broke. "Remember the story I told you: how the ancient Egyptians back on Earth cut themselves off from Ra? That is exactly what you have to do." He took a deep breath and looked up again at the Gate. "Then in one year—one year from this day, you take the cover stone away. I will try to bring Sha're home on that day. But if I don't make it back, if I don't return, you must bury the Gate again. Forever." He swallowed, then asked for their assent in their own language. *"Joa qua?"*

The boy, hugging him fiercely, nodded, fighting back tears. As the Earth team watched, the people of Abydos moved in around Daniel and the boy, hugging the scientist, burying him in touches meant to reassure both giver and receiver.

"Tell Sha're's father"—Daniel's voice became stronger, more fervent as he made a promise of his own—"in *one year* . . .

"Promise me," Daniel went on. "All of you."

A murmur rose from the assembled people, a reluctant assent.

"We promise, Dani-el," the boy said, speaking for them all.

In the Gate room on Earth, soldiers milled about in purposeful activity, setting up defenses. Machine-gun emplacements were sandbagged and ready, extra belts of ammunition were in place, and a few special surprises had been added. As the room began to rumble, Samuels and Hammond looked up from their inspection. The inner ring of the Gate began to move.

Instantly alarms sounded, and a voice boomed over the loudspeaker. "Stand by for arrival! Stand by for arrival!"

The now familiar funnel of light formed and retracted, stabilized. Through the Gate came Colonel O'Neill, carrying a bloody uniformed body as if cradling a sleeping child. After him came Kawalsky, staggering under the weight of what were obviously bodies over his shoulder, followed by Carter and a scruffy-looking, bespectacled young man whose face was white and immobile with grief. O'Neill went immediately to the nearest table and laid his burden on it.

As soon as they were clear of the Gate, Samuels barked, "Close the iris!"

An engineer pushed a button. What was left of the team spun around, guns ready, at the sound of shrieking metal. As they watched, a sharp-edged metal iris spiraled shut over the Gate, sealing it.

O'Neill, next to the table, looked at the general, surprised. "What the hell's that?"

"That's our insurance against any more surprises," the general informed him. "Little idea I got from Jackson's barricade. Pure titanium, hopefully impenetrable." He looked over the casualties, and his eyes became grim. "What happened, Colonel?"

"Base camp got hit while we were on recon," O'Neill said briefly. "Ferretti's down." One hand strayed unconsciously to touch the injured man, as if to reassure him. Medics scrambled to get Ferretti on a gurney, to relieve Kawalsky of his grisly burdens.

"Same hostiles who attacked us?"

O'Neill nodded. "Best guess. Jackson's wife and one of my kids were kidnapped."

The phrasing gave the general pause. "*Your* kids?"

"From the first mission, sir—"

Jackson broke in, unable to wait any longer. "General? Hi, um, Daniel Jackson, we've never met. I'd like to be on the team that goes after them."

Hammond looked the young archaeologist over. He wasn't sure he liked what he saw—a long-haired, bespectacled young man dressed in wool robes and smelling of goat. "You're not in any position to make demands, Jackson."

Jackson flinched and fell silent.

The gurney was wheeled out of the room. The reconnaissance team and the general followed.

"Sir," O'Neill told him, "we know the hostiles didn't come from Abydos. But Daniel found evidence that there's a whole network of Stargates out there—all over the galaxy. They could be anywhere."

That news stopped Hammond in his tracks. *"Network?"*

Carter spoke up. "We think Ferretti saw the sequence of symbols they used to go through the Stargate. That should tell us where they went. General, Dr. Jackson found a room on Abydos with a thousand possible coordinates, maybe more. That's a thousand new worlds, General!"

"And our Stargate can take us to these *worlds*?" The general was having trouble grasping the scope of the idea. Not for lack of imagination, but out of a stunned realization that the problems presented by the one known Stargate had just been multiplied a thousandfold.

Maybe more. Between that and the heavy casualties, he was not a happy general.

"With this new data, sir, as long as we make the appropriate allowances for alignment in the targeting computer—"

"Yes or no?"

"I think so, sir, yes. Request permission to upload the symbols into the base supercomputer for analysis."

O'Neill broke back in, a feral urgency in his eyes. "General, I assume I'll be leading the rescue mission once we find out the hostiles' location—"

Hammond raised his hand for silence.

"All right, people, all right. There will be a debriefing at 0800 hours, after I've had a chance to confer with my superiors about this new . . . situation. Captain Carter, the base computer is at your disposal." To O'Neill he added, "Colonel, we'll discuss your request at the briefing." He wasn't making any promises. "In the meantime"—he indicated Daniel with a jerk of his head—"get this man a clean uniform. He stinks."

The general spun around and marched off, heading for the nearest secure phone. Carter followed him, unlimbering her video recorder. Jackson and O'Neill stood staring after them, and then back at the Gate through which they had just come.

"Don't worry," O'Neill said softly. "We'll find them, Daniel."

Elsewhere, somewhere unimaginable among the stars, Skaara and his sister Sha're stood within a massive prison building, an arena full of people. The building was made of great blocks of stone, with fluted columns. At one end was a high, arched door made of thick metal bars. Skaara and Sha're shivered, as much from the aftereffects of their terrifying journey through the wormhole as from sheer terror.

The people around them were not normal people of Abydos; their skin and hair were of all colors. Some wore animal skins with patterns they had never seen before, and some, strange shiny cloth. They were all afraid too, huddled together and whispering in their fear.

Skaara stood in front of Sha're to protect her, though no one seemed very interested in them. The air was thick, dense with an unfamiliar level of humidity; it seemed tinted purple, like the shell of a dung beetle, and was hard to breathe.

Through the door came a line of many Serpent Guards, holding the death sticks.

One of them stepped forward. His snake helmet was folded down; the two of them recognized him as the one the Ra-god had called Teal'c. Teal'c pointed to Sha're and said to her sharply, "*Chek mok!*"

Skaara moved between them, and the guard accompanying Teal'c aimed a death stick at him. Skaara swallowed, frightened, but lifted his head in defiance anyway. Sha're was his sister and Daniel's beloved. Daniel was not here to protect her, so the responsibility fell to him.

The dark man spoke to him as if in sympathy. "Your death cannot help her."

Skaara was startled by the sound of his own language, and by the look in the man's eyes. This Teal'c seemed almost human. Still, he served the Ra-god, the accursed one. . . .

Sha're put a hand on her brother's arm. "No, Skaara." To Teal'c she added bravely, "I am not afraid."

One of the Serpent Guards led her away, one of many that the devil ones selected out of the crowd. Muffled cries of grief followed them as other families were torn apart. Skaara lunged forward, wild with helplessness, but was stopped, held back by other prisoners.

Teal'c paused, looking back, and gave Skaara a nod, as if acknowledging that the boy had made a brave effort. Frustrated, enraged, the boy watched his sister walk out the arched door, her head high and proud, like a queen.

Late that night, O'Neill, cleaned up and inexpressibly weary, stopped by the infirmary to see the surviving member of the firefight in the Abydos Gate room. Louis Ferretti was lying on a cot, the upper half of his body and one side of his face heavily bandaged. Tubes eeled out of all parts of his body. Throbbing lights over the bed recorded respiration, heartbeat. One arm was hung from a metal contraption. The place stank of antiseptic and sickness.

Beside him, hunched over, sat Kawalsky, staring at his folded hands.

"They tell me he's gonna make it," O'Neill said softly. He had no reason to doubt it; this might be a secret base, but he'd seen how this place was outfitted, and it put many military hospitals to shame.

Kawalsky nodded, never taking his eyes from his twisted fingers. "Yes, sir."

It didn't matter. Ferretti was one of *his men*, damn it, and he took the man's injuries, and the deaths of the others involved, very, very personally.

The fact that the injuries and deaths couldn't stop the kidnapping of Daniel's wife, of the boy he had adopted for his own, made it that much worse.

"You gonna stay here all night?"

"Yes, sir."

O'Neill nodded quietly. That was Kawalsky's right and privilege. O'Neill might be Ferretti's commanding officer, but Kawalsky was his best friend. He gave the patient one last look and stepped back out into the corridor.

At the end of the hall, looking around as if not at all sure what direction to take or even why, stood Daniel Jackson. He was wearing a fresh, clean set of fatigues that looked far too big for him. O'Neill stopped in front of him and waited patiently for the other man to notice him.

"They don't know what to do with me." Jackson's voice was bewildered. Lost. He smiled quickly, blinking through the lenses of his glasses.

O'Neill nodded again. At least this one of his stray sheep he could do something about. "C'mon. Let's get outta here." With a jerk of his head, he gathered the other man up to follow him.

In the middle of examining the display of commendations and citations and photographs decorating the wall and mantelpiece of the fireplace in Jack O'Neill's living room, Jackson sneezed.

"Bless you." O'Neill passed him a box of tissues. They were drinking; at least, O'Neill was drinking, working on his second or third beer. Jackson was still nursing his first. Despite Skaara's experiments, he was clearly unused to alcohol. His words were a little unsteady.

"Going from one planet to another makes my allergies—" He blew his nose, stopped to think about what he'd just said, shrugged.

"Anyway. As soon as you were gone and they realized they were *free*—I mean, Abydos was their world for the taking—"

"You have a party?" O'Neill was watching him, faculties unblurred by the liquor.

"Oh, big, big party. They treated me like their savior, it was . . ." He blushed. "Embarrassing."

O'Neill raised a bottle in ironic salute, slid back deep into the tan leather couch. "Daniel Jackson. Savior of Abydos. It's amazing you turned out so normal."

Jackson smiled, a tentative, sweet expression, and took the chair opposite, setting his bottle down on the coffee table. "I spent the first year having to stop everyone I saw from bowing all the time. It was like, 'Hi, please don't do that.'. . ." He blushed and picked up the bottle again, taking a swig of beer.

"Lucky it didn't go to your head."

Jackson laughed, as if at a memory of himself. "If it wasn't for Sha're, I . . . She was the complete opposite of everyone else. She practically . . . fell on the floor laughing every time I tried to do some chore they all took for granted. Like . . . grinding *yaphetta* flour. Have you ever tried to grind your own flour?"

O'Neill opened another beer. "Actually, I'm trying to kick the flour thing."

Daniel drained the last swallow. "This is going straight to my head. What time is it, anyway? I must have Gate lag."

O'Neill laughed. "You've had *one* beer, Daniel. You're a cheaper date than my wife was."

Jackson grasped foggily at the change of subject and gestured broadly at the frames on the wall and the stone mantelpiece. Photographs of O'Neill with a woman were conspicuously absent. Come to think of it, he thought fuzzily, the room did have a rather Spartan look about it. It was painfully neat, done in shades of tan and brown, and there wasn't a copy of *Good Housekeeping* anywhere. All the carpet seemed brand-new. "Yeah, when am I going to meet your wife?"

O'Neill snorted. "Oh, probably . . . never. When I came back from Abydos the first time, she'd already left."

Daniel stared at him, eyes owlish behind the wire-rimmed lenses. "I'm sorry."

O'Neill's mouth twitched, and he swirled the liquid in the brown bottle. "Yeah." Taking a deep breath, he went on, "So was I. But I guess saying it didn't change anything." He took a deep drink. "I think in her heart she forgave me for what happened to our kid; she just . . . wasn't able to forget."

Jackson blinked earnestly. "And what about you?"

An edge of sober harshness entered O'Neill's voice. "Me, I'm the opposite. I'll *never* forgive myself." He took another long swallow of beer. "But sometimes I can forget."

Daniel picked up his bottle again and rolled it back and forth between his palms, watching the other man, trying to think of something to say that wouldn't seem trite or sentimental. He wondered if O'Neill was telling the truth about being about to forget; he doubted it. But about not being able to forgive himself, well, that part was true. He could tell that just by the look in O'Neill's eyes when he had realized Skaara was gone too. There were a lot of things, it seemed, that Jack O'Neill would never forgive himself for.

* * *

Sergeant Carol Ketering watched as one of the new ones slid a small loaf of bread from one of the silver platters into her diaphanous gown. The woman was thinking of escape, then. Ketering could have told her there was no way out of this—this harem; she had tried all the doors, meeting stolid human guards or, worse, the Snakeheads each time, and there were no windows in the stone walls. Just luxury, flowing transparent gowns, vessels of gold and silver, incense, wine. Slave boys dressed only in twisted loincloths providing massages. Sweet-scented violet air.

Everything a woman could want, in fact.

Except freedom. Carol Ketering believed very strongly in freedom.

They had taken away her uniform, the khaki pants, tank top, jacket. They'd shoved her toward a perfumed bath, pointed at a diaphanous pile of white, nearly transparent silks. Men and women she could only think of as slaves had bathed her, washed her hair. After a while she'd submitted, telling herself that there was no point in exhausting herself struggling against taking a hot bath.

She watched the human guards tensing.

He was coming again, then. They always stood to attention when Teal'c came. It didn't take much to recognize the hierarchy.

And when Teal'c came, someone always left with him. Carol moved back, stealthily, hoping to avoid notice. Several of the others around her did the same. The new one, though, not yet up on the protocol, merely looked around apprehensively. For a moment her eyes, dark and bright, met Carol's, and despite any differences in the worlds of their respective births, a flash of perfect understanding passed between them. The new woman too faded back into the crowd.

Unfortunately, when everyone was pressing back trying not to be noticed, *someone* always ended up still in front.

Teal'c pointed with his staff.

Take her, Carol thought without shame as the staff appeared to waver toward someone else. *Take her, not me.*

But the staff *was* pointing at her after all. The slaves moved forward. Carol stood, contempt clear in her face. She was in the United States Air Force, by God, and she wasn't going to let them get anything out of her but her name, rank, and serial number.

As soon as they grabbed her, the facade crumbled.

"Where are you taking me? I'm a sergeant in the United States Air Force, and I demand to know where you're taking me!"

Ignoring her struggles, Teal'c grabbed her wrist and dragged her along, down the dark halls. The escort marched close behind. Even if she had managed to break free, there was nowhere to go.

Finally they entered a huge room lit by a fire roaring in a brazier. The high walls were draped in gauze-like linen. The heat made her sweat. So did the sight of the man the other women called the Lord Apophis, whispering dread stories behind their hands every time one of their number was taken, never to return.

As she had been taken.

He was wearing a gold skullcap, gold kilt and sandals, and his collar was covered with jasper and turquoise. Bracelets twined around his wrists and hands. His body shone as if oiled.

Apophis studied her as she screamed and

kicked, fighting with every fiber of her being, wild with a certain knowledge that death stood before her. "Let me go!"

Then he reached out and touched her forehead, the stone in his palms glowing, and suddenly she wasn't struggling anymore. There was fear, but it was very very far away.

"Lovely," he said in deep, guttural voice. "You could be the vessel for my future queen."

Queen? She wondered numbly. Deep inside, a part of her mind that remained her own began a steady screaming.

He walked around her, looking her over like a prize mare, and snapped his fingers. Two more slaves stepped out of the shadows, light gleaming off the knives in their hands.

Carol saw the glitter, wondered at it, and did not move.

The slaves cut away her clothing, leaving her naked. Apophis caressed her, smiling, touching her all over her body, leaning over to sniff her skin, walking around her as if inspecting a particularly fine cut of meat.

"Yes," the guttural voice said. "Yes, very nice indeed. But I am not the one you must finally please."

He wanted her to lie on the stone slab before the brazier, she understood, without knowing how she understood it. She lay relaxed, looking up, seeing Teal'c, seeing Apophis. Teal'c was impassive, as if he had seen this many times before. The sliver of self that remained to her gibbered with fear.

She saw a lovely woman come from the shadows, her gown flowing loosely around her. The woman wore long robes, heavily embroidered, and a veil over her face. Through the transparent cloth Carol could see that her skin was very fair, and her dark eyes brimmed with sympathy, kindness, wisdom.

"*Yametha. Re!*" the lord said.

The woman stood beside the stone slab and parted her garments to reveal her upper belly—and the slit that gaped in it. The opening pulsed in and out.

Carol watched, breathing evenly, screaming inside, as something thick and white snaked out of the slit in the woman's body. Far from expressing pain, the woman leaned back her head, an expression of ecstasy crossing her face.

The thing dripped something vile and viscous across Carol's skin as its head twisted and shifted, more and more of the translucent body issuing forth, as it investigated her intimately. Its jaws split in three, and winglets stood out behind them. It made a noise.

Apophis watched eagerly.

The thing came up into her face. If it had had eyes, she would have said it stared at her.

Again it made a noise, a shrill screech of rejection, and abruptly it withdrew, retracting into the woman's belly. She gasped once, as if with pleasure, then slowly closed her robe.

"A shame," the lord said as the woman returned to the shadows. His hand came out to stroke Carol's forehead again, the device upon his hand glowing.

As the remaining independent spark of Sergeant Carol Ketering struggled and flickered, she saw the lord's eyes glow, heard his last words as if from far away, and the scrap that was Carol fled them, into the final safety of ultimate darkness and refuge from horror.

"Send another," Apophis said.

And Carol was grateful to die.

CHAPTER SEVEN

"Ten-hut!" Samuels barked in an excellent imitation of a drill sergeant. In response, the others seated around the briefing table came to attention as General Hammond entered.

The general moved to the head of the table and remained standing, resting his knuckles against the polished wood. All the dust covers were gone now. All the equipment was fully functional.

"People, what is spoken of in this room is classified NSI Top Secret," he announced. Then, with a sharp look at O'Neill, he went on, "Colonel. What do we know about these hostiles that we didn't know yesterday?"

O'Neill barely refrained from an unmilitary shrug. "Not a helluva lot, sir. The Abydos boys who survived the attack on our base camp believed it was Ra."

"I thought he was dead, gentlemen. Which is it?"

"Oh, he's dead. He's definitely dead," Jackson said, polishing his glasses. He looked at O'Neill. "The bomb . . . I mean, he has to be dead, right?"

O'Neill closed his eyes to keep from rolling them too obviously.

"Then who is coming through the Stargate?" Hammond snapped.

Jackson cocked his head, thinking. With an air of a thinker reaching a satisfactory conclusion he piped up, "Gods."

This was not what Hammond had expected. "What?" The word was nothing if not the roar of the enraged bull general.

"Not as in *God* Gods," Jackson explained, tumbling back into a professor persona without skipping a beat. "Ra *played* a god—the sun god. He 'borrowed' the religion and culture of the ancient Egyptians he brought through the Gate and then used it to enslave them. He wanted the people of Abydos to believe he was the only one."

Carter, with professorial tendencies herself, caught on. "You're saying Ra wasn't the last of his race after all."

"Maybe he's got a brother, Ray," Kawalsky quipped sourly.

"*That's* what we need," O'Neill muttered, agreeing with him.

Daniel was off in full cry after a theory. "Wait a minute. The legend goes, Ra's race was dying. . . . *He* survived by taking over the body of his human host, an Egyptian boy. But who's to say more of his kind couldn't do the same thing? They could have done it anytime and"—the impact of his own words sank in—"*anywhere there's a Gate.*" He paled. "It could be happening . . . now."

Hammond took it in and turned to O'Neill. "Colonel, you've had the most experience in fighting this hostile. Assuming you have to defend yourself in the field—are you up to it?"

O'Neill's lips tightened. "We beat 'em once."

Hammond looked at him. "I'll take that as a maybe." Shifting his attention, he went on, "Captain Carter, you're confident our Stargate will send us where we want to go with this new information?"

Carter showed signs of a very long night. "The computer's feeding revised coordinates to the targeting computer now. It'll take time to calculate, but it should spit out two or three destinations a month."

Hammond nodded, taking a deep breath. "People, let's not fool ourselves here. This thing is both vast and dangerous, and we are so far over our heads we can barely see daylight. These hostiles we're up against possess technology so far superior to our own, we don't have the faintest idea how it works.

"We would all be much better off if the Stargate had been left in the ground."

Carter protested. "With respect, sir, we can't bury our heads in the sand. Think of how much we could learn! Think of what we could bring back—"

Hammond had had enough of the upstart captain. "*What you could bring back* is precisely what I'm afraid of, Captain," he roared. "However . . ."—he forced himself to swallow his ire—"the President of the United States happens to agree with you. In the event your theories pan out, he's ordered the formation of nine teams whose duties will be to perform reconnaissance, determine threats, and if possible, to make peaceful contact with the peoples of these worlds. These teams will operate on a covert, top-secret basis. No one will know of their existence except the President and the Joint Chiefs.

"Colonel O'Neill."

O'Neill blinked. "Sir."

"Your team will be designated SG-1. The team will consist of yourself, Captain Carter—"

"And me," Jackson interrupted. His hands were twisted together in a knot on the gleaming table.

Hammond shook his head. "Dr. Jackson, we need you to work as a consultant with the other SG teams from here. Your expertise in ancient cultures and languages are far too valuable—"

"No," Jackson insisted, and tried to soften it with a quick, pleading smile. "I mean, I know this is your decision. I just . . . I really have to be on *their* team." He leaned forward, trying to make the general understand. "My *wife* is out there, General. I need to go."

Hammond's look was troubled. Clearly he sympathized, but there was miliary necessity too. "I'll take that under consideration," he said at last, unwilling to deny Jackson completely. "Major Kawalsky, you'll head SG-2."

"I will?" Kawalsky gaped, caught flat-footed.

"Colonel O'Neill says it's about time you had a command."

Kawalsky swiveled to look at the colonel, who shrugged and said, "I had a moment of weakness."

As he spoke, an aide entered and whispered in Major Samuels' ear. Smiling, he repeated it. "Ferretti's conscious, sir."

Ignoring protocol, O'Neill lunged for the door. He was gone before Hammond could finish saying, "Dismissed."

Carter seemed disposed to shove the medic out of the way as they entered the sickroom. "I'll take over, thanks," she said, and moved in beside the injured man's pillow.

Ferretti was in good spirits, possibly because he was doped to the gills and too groggy to notice the tubes sticking out of him. He tried to smile around the respirator at O'Neill and Kawalsky, and even tried to wink with his unbandaged eye at Carter. A technician set up a bed tray beside the bed, careful not to brush against the patient, and placed a laptop computer on it, tilting the screen so Ferretti could see. Carter hit the keys to start her program running.

"Listen, Ferretti, I know you're probably not feeling so hot, but we need something from you."

Carter glanced at the colonel, surprised at the compassion and iron need in his voice. Ignoring her, O'Neill shifted to make it easier for the patient to move his hand.

On the laptop screen, the symbols of the Abydos Gate blinked on in slow succession. Ferretti pointed a trembling hand at one of them.

"Looks like he's way ahead of you, Colonel," Carter observed.

O'Neill continued to ignore her, focused completely on Ferretti. "You saw all seven symbols? You sure this is where they went?"

Ferretti nodded, gesturing to bring the screen closer so he could point more easily.

"Good eye, Major," O'Neill said, smiling at him.

It took a long time, and when Ferretti was finished he was shaking with exhaustion. But they had all seven symbols, in the correct order. God willing, it would take them to Skaara and Sha're.

The team was dressed in battle fatigues, waiting as the Gate spun for its new destination. In addition to regular battle kit—the uniform of the day was jungle camouflage for some reason—they had a motorized battle cart. The cart, the size of a sport-utility vehicle without the top half, was loaded with weapons and ammunition as well as other, more mundane supplies. Stenciled on its side was the cryptic acronym FRED.

Kawalsky had personally made sure that there was lots and *lots* of extra ammunition.

In the background, technicians did mysterious things, and they could hear a voice announcing, "Chevron five, encoded."

Samuels, looking smart and crisp and every inch the desk jockey, gave them last-minute instructions.

"Colonel, I want to remind you that rescuing Dr. Jackson's wife is a secondary objective. In the event you fail to return to base camp within twenty-four hours, SG-2 will scrub the mission and return without you."

"Understood," O'Neill said, expressionless.

Kawalsky snorted. "Not gonna happen, Colonel. SG-2 won't leave without you."

Samuels gave him an affronted glare.

Behind him a loudspeaker announced, "Chevron Six, encoded."

Samuels decided to ignore Kawalsky. He held up a wrist remote-control device. "All right. Let's confirm transmitter codes."

Carter and Kawalsky pulled back their sleeves and showed Samuels the devices on their own wrists. The room began shaking, and Samuels had to raise his voice. "I want to remind you that only the right code will open the iris. If you lose the transmitter, you cannot get home."

O'Neill, watching the Gate, was no longer even pretending to pay attention to him. Carter answered for him. "Understood, sir."

"Chevron seven, *locked*."

"Clear!"

The team shifted, eager to follow the retreating funnel up the ramp.

Over the loudspeaker Hammond's voice

sounded hollow as he repeated his warning. "SG-1 and SG-2, if you do not return in twenty-four hours, your remote transmitter codes will be locked out and the iris will be sealed permanently. At that point there will be no return. *Is that understood?*"

"Yes, sir," O'Neill snapped. Then, to the team, "Let's move out."

The troops lined up and started up the ramp. As O'Neill and Kawalsky passed Samuels, they heard him mutter, "Wish I was going with you."

The colonel and the major exchanged a look. O'Neill managed to keep his mouth shut. Kawalsky didn't. "Yeah? I'm kinda glad you're staying behind."

CHAPTER EIGHT

O'Neill hit the ground rolling, feeling the bite of gravel through his jacket. The cold of the trip through the Gate had chilled him to the bone and left a rime of frost on his eyelashes. He muttered a curse, brushing it away, and looked around, taking stock of their position and accounting for his team. Everyone seemed to be okay, but FRED the battle cart seemed to have landed half on top of a boulder.

Kawalsky catapulted out of the Gate, hit the ground, and snarled, "*Damn* it's cold!"

O'Neill didn't disagree, but that wasn't the point. "Okay, people, get our gear out. Let's move, move!"

They were in a large wooded clearing, with a centerpiece of the Gate and a stone altar standing before it. The clearing looked like a miniature Stonehenge, with rings of small boulders, set carefully on end, surrounding the centerpiece. It was a new world, a new planet; the trees were different somehow. O'Neill firmly quashed the temptation to gawk. They were in enemy territory, and the fact that it was a different world didn't matter. Their strategic goals were defined, and tactics were tactics anywhere in the galaxy.

So far they had retained the element of surprise. The soldiers deployed in defensive perimeter were alert and ready. They needed to get organized, be ready to defend themselves. . . .

Daniel sneezed. "Anybody have a Kleenex?" he asked, for all the world as if he were back home in the briefing room.

O'Neill glared at him. *Scientists!*

Sha're sat by a wall, next to a fluted column, uneasily plucking the unfamiliar fabric of her gown. On a marble table nearby, another woman luxuriated in an oil rubdown. The other women were sampling delicacies from silver platters and talking among themselves;

she could understand some of them, at least a word or two here and there. Sha're wasn't hungry, and even if she was she couldn't bring herself to try the food of the Ra-gods and serpent soldiers.

The main subject of discussion was what had happened to the strange blond woman taken by the Serpent Guards. Many were afraid. Some were envious. They speculated eagerly about where she had gone.

When the Serpent Guards returned, those were the women who pushed forward, who postured before them, smiling, flirting, caressing. The Guards ignored them, scanning the crowd intently. Sha're turned her back to them, refusing to acknowledge their existence. Since being separated from her brother and brought to this house of women, she had felt desperately alone.

"You!" one said, pointing directly at Sha're. She could feel his gaze on her, hear the movement of the other women as they moved out of the path of the guards. *No*, she thought desperately, *not me. Daniel, Skaara, where are you*?

Out of the corner of her eye she could see them coming, and could no longer deny that she was the focus of their attention. Horrified, she bolted, shoving her way past the disappointed volunteers, but the slaves grabbed her.

Sha're screamed in denial, refusal. She kicked and fought.

It made no difference.

This time they had everything they wished they'd had before: mines, Stingers, infrared, everything O'Neill and Kawalsky could think of. O'Neill decided he'd feel better about it if he was more convinced they'd thought of enough.

Jackson, of course, simply sat cross-legged on a crate and watched the military do all the real work. He had his arms crossed, hugging himself—trying to keep warm. He could have kept warm by doing something useful, the colonel thought sourly, but no. How many calories can you burn by just thinking?

"It must be some sort of ceremonial place. The gate is—*has* to be—an integral part of their spiritual culture." Catching O'Neil's eye, he nodded to the arrangement before the Gate. "See? That's an altar of some kind. This place was built for worshipers."

Back in college O'Neill had heard a joke

once: how come archaeologists can always identify all the junk they dig up? Because anything they can't identify is obviously a ceremonial object.

"Let's just be on our way before the *worshipees* show up."

Jackson looked confused.

O'Neill changed tack. "You figure out yet how to align this Gate to get back home?"

Jackson nodded eagerly. "Yes, of course. The device is the same as on Abydos." He hopped off the crate and pointed at the altar. The symbols surrounding the center stone were beginning to look very familiar. "This symbol represents—"

O'Neill interrupted. "Have you briefed Kawalsky's team yet?"

Jackson tried again. "Yes. This symbol—"

"Good enough." Jackson couldn't get it through his well-meaning, fuzzy scientific head that O'Neill didn't *care* about the esoteric meanings of the Gate symbols; he wanted to make sure his line of retreat was open, period. This wasn't the time or place for lectures.

Kawalsky came step-wise down the slope, gesturing to an area of trees. "We'll set up camp down there, where there's better cover. I've found a trail on the mountain that looks like it's seen traffic in the last couple of days."

O'Neill looked over the proposed site for the second team's base camp and approved. "We'd better start down. . . . Where's Carter?"

As he spoke, thinking irritated thoughts about scientists again, Carter showed up out of the trees, calling to Kawalsky, "I set up a line of claymores along that ridge at intervals of ten meters and wired them back to the Gate."

O'Neill raised an eyebrow. On the other hand, a *bloodthirsty* scientist might actually come in handy. There might be hope for Carter yet. "That sound about right, Kawalsky?"

Kawalsky chortled. "Yeah, that'll work."

The rest of SG-2 moved up, and Kawalsky directed them to the chosen camp site. The two officers watched for a few moments, and then, satisfied that things were going well, O'Neill got back to business. "Okay. If we're not back in twenty hours—"

"We'll come and rescue your sorry asses," Kawalsky said jauntily.

O'Neill stared at him. "You'll go back through the gate with the combination Daniel just gave you, before the iris is locked so you *can't* go back." The tone of his voice brooked no argument.

Kawalsky looked as if he wanted to argue anyway, but swallowed instead. "Yes, sir."

"If we don't make it back, we got our butt kicked, and that means you tuck tail." O'Neill wasn't about to let Kawalsky have any latitude at all in interpreting his orders. That was a privilege he reserved for himself, and besides, he had no intention of letting Kawalsky end up in the same shape Ferretti was in.

The frozen tête-à-tête was broken by a member of O'Neill's team, an Airman Warren.

"Sirs, I found what looks like a trail down the mountain. Looks like it's seen traffic in the last couple of days."

Time to go. "Thank you, Airman." He gave Kawalsky one last look. "Hold the fort."

"Bring me back a T-shirt."

Where the hell did Kawalsky pick up an attitude like that? O'Neill wondered as they traded salutes and headed downslope in the direction Warren indicated.

Sha're fought savagely, but there were two Serpent Guards and two slave boys, and all her twisting and shrieking was for nothing.

Apophis entered through a gap in the curtains. Sha're redoubled her struggles. The Ragod watched, plainly amused. His eyes glittered under the kohl. "This one has spirit," he observed, snapping his fingers to the slave boys.

They reached for the straps of her dress, and she snapped, her teeth sinking into flesh. Apophis laughed at the boy's scream, and reached forward with the hand wrapped in the glowing serpent device.

It was . . . as if nothing mattered anymore. She felt remote, distant, as if watching something happening to someone else, someone who didn't matter to her. Someone who was stripped naked to stand before the golden one. A part of her was very afraid, but it was far away.

"Does she please you, my love?"

She could hear the words, understand them, but they didn't matter.

She could see a tall, beautiful woman step out of the shadows and move close; she could see the snakelike creature protruding out of the slit in the woman's belly. The snake was whining to itself, making a painful, high-pitched sound, writhing, stretching itself to come closer to the disinterested body that was Sha're.

Apophis signaled again, and the guards and slaves lifted her, placed her on an elaborate altar. The woman came close.

The snake slithered clear of its host, onto Sha're's belly. She could feel the weight of it, the cold slime, the little touches of its—teeth?—about her body, between her breasts. Up to the nape of her neck. Poking at her insistently.

The slaves rolled her over onto her stomach. She could feel the snake crawling down her back, to the base of her spine, as if examining each vertebra. Out of the corner of her eye she could see the expression of joy, of blissful happiness on Apophis's face. The other woman sighed, as if in regret, and closing her robes, she moved away, back into the shadows.

She could feel part of the weight of the thing lift itself, as if it were rearing up. . . .

And she screamed as the snake plunged into her neck, entering her, forcing the outer Sha're and the inner, terrified one back together as it took possession of them both.

CHAPTER NINE

SG-1 moved down a steep path in the forest, O'Neill in the lead. Daniel Jackson was still shivering.

"Do we have any idea where we're going?" he asked.

"Down, Daniel," O'Neill said patiently.

"Get your mind off the cold," Carter suggested. After a moment she added, "Tell me about Sha're."

Oh, good grief, O'Neill thought.

"Well," Daniel said intelligently, catching himself as he slipped in the mud, "she's, um . . ."

"She was a gift," O'Neill said wickedly.

Carter made a shocked noise.

"She *was,*" Jackson said, protesting. "From

the elders of Abydos the first night we were there."

"And you *accepted*?" Carter was outraged.

Daniel shrugged: *Of course, what could I do*?

O'Neill, having set this particular cat among the pigeons, was more than willing to enjoy the carnage, but he kept his mind on his job too.

"Hold up!"

"What?" Daniel was confused. Apparently, O'Neill thought, the archaeologist was under the impression they were going for a simple walk in the park.

Carter grabbed Daniel more or less by the scruff of the neck and pulled him behind a huge log. The Captain Doctor really did have potential after all.

As they took cover, a line of—monks?— made their way up the path past them. At least, they looked like monks; there were six or eight of them, wearing heavy hooded robes. O'Neill slipped the safety off his weapon.

The lead monk stopped at the place Jackson had slipped, pointing it out to the others. Their voices rose in consternation.

"D'you see any weapons?" O'Neill asked softly.

"No, sir," Carter responded.

Daniel sat up, fortunately still out of the sight of the monks. "They're worshipers."

Ignoring him, O'Neill said, "Captain, take a position fifty yards up—"

Ignoring the scientist was a bad habit he really should have broken a long time ago. Jackson was on his feet, walking out onto the path with his arms wide open. "Hi!"

O'Neill closed his eyes in despair. "The man has not changed."

Jackson was still talking. "We just, um, we just came through the Stargate. The *chaapa'ai.*"

The monks pulled back their hoods. All men, fairly old; they looked harmless, except for the gold markings on their foreheads that were identical to those on the foreheads of the Serpent Guards. Then again, Jackson looked harmless too, and he was probably the biggest loose cannon on the planet.

The lead monk smiled. "Stargate?" He was tentative, as if making sure he'd heard this odd stranger correctly. *"Chaapa'ai?"*

Jackson nodded vigorously. "Stargate, that's right." Holding out his hand, he repeated, "Hi!"

The monks fell to their knees before him.

Jackson's hand dropped. "No, no," he said desperately, "please don't do that. . . ." He tried to make them get up, without notable success.

O'Neill got up, his hand still on his sidearm. "How'd you know they'd react this way?"

"I didn't." He was still smiling, trying to make friends. "But unless we want to get ourselves a really bad reputation, I think we should avoid shooting the first people we meet on a new planet." He helped the confused head monk to his feet. "Please, you don't have to do this."

"You come to choose?" the monk asked.

Jackson, baffled, looked to O'Neill. "Choose?"

O'Neill shrugged. He was still thinking about the fine line between getting a bad reputation and conducting a straightforward military invasion.

"Sure, we can choose. Choosing is good," Jackson decided. Ever the pedant, he informed O'Neill, "It's a derivation of Arabic combined with—"

"Yeah, yeah, just ask them to take us to the

nearest city," O'Neill suggested. As long as Jackson was so set on communicating, he might as well get directions.

Somehow it didn't surprise O'Neill that Jackson had no trouble asking directions. The archaeologist smiled again at the monk. "Would you take us—?" At the same time he held up his hands, fingertips together to form a steeply pitched roof.

Every time O'Neill had ever even *considered* asking for directions, he'd found his way almost immediately, making the discomfort of asking totally unnecessary. He *hated* asking for directions. Jackson, on the other hand, had no trouble at all asking, and the monks had no trouble answering. They nodded eagerly to Jackson. "We take you. Yes. Come."

The monks led them around a bank of trees and swept an arm out, displaying a wide vista, a valley at the foot of the mountain, a valley filled from one end to the other with a city.

"Chulak. Yes?"

The human team was awestruck, each for their own reasons. O'Neill was appalled at the sheer size of the place. What if it was *full* of Ra-aliens?

"Chulak sounds good," Jackson stammered at last. "Yes. Chulak."

The rest of the monks hauled themselves to their feet and prepared to lead them down the path.

"I hear it's nice this time of year," O'Neill muttered.

O'Neill had had occasion from time to time to pass through Rome on his way to bases in Germany, Turkey, Spain. In his off hours he had enjoyed wandering through the Eternal City, trading wry observations with the cats in the Coliseum, looking over the triumphal arches and broken marble statues of long-dead emperors. Chulak reminded him of that city, perhaps as it might have been a thousand years ago. The same wide boulevards branched out into narrow little twisting streets with laundry hanging out the windows, ripe smells hanging like a miasma in rubbled corners. The same marble columns, in less disrepair, graced the monuments. It looked like the kind of place a man could find a halfway decent bar but no ice.

"Everyone looks so . . . human," Carter murmured.

Human, but with no fashion sense. The people of Chulak all wore the same kind of robes. The Earth team got stares, as much for their fatigues as their obvious alienness.

Well, everybody in ancient Rome probably wore togas.

"Maybe they are . . . or were." Jackson was answering Carter. O'Neill gave him a look. Jackson shrugged a little. "The people of Abydos were separated from the rest of humanity for five thousand years. Societies can evolve a lot in that time."

They just hadn't gotten around to evolving a Versace or Armani yet.

If this really had been Rome, the building they were approaching now would be the Vatican. It wasn't domed, though. The monks escorted them up a grand stone staircase, through vast doors, and into a room with two levels, the lower one set up for a royal banquet. Up a couple of steps, the rest of the room was empty except for doors at the other end. The head monk turned and bowed to them, gesturing to the food displayed on the long table, and made an unintelligible introduction. The people already present made room for them, giving their strange attire no more than a casual glance. Their attention seemed to be on the doorways, not the food.

"Why are they treating us like this?" Carter said, nervously fingering her rifle.

Jackson was looking around as if seeking someone particular. "They think we're gods," he said absently.

"Incredible."

"Okay, we're gods. Now what?" When Carter glared at him, O'Neill shrugged nonchalantly. "Happens all the time." A group of women wearing nothing much were hovering, eyeing the newcomers. O'Neill eyed them back appreciatively.

"This is a ceremony of some kind," Jackson said suddenly. "We've been expected."

O'Neill was still appreciating. "All right, if we're gods, what're we supposed to *choose*?"

"I have no idea."

Somewhere back in the shadows someone struck a gong, and O'Neill dropped all pretense of being on vacation. "Okay, Daniel, I think we should tell them we want to look around—"

He stopped as a pair of Serpent Guards entered the room, carrying large, twisted horns that looked like they might have been made of animal tusks.

The Guards took up ceremonial positions and blew the horns. The monkish escort fell to their knees, bowing their heads to the stone floor. All the rest of the people at the table moved away and also fell to their knees. After a moment Jackson did the same, looking around at O'Neill and Carter.

"When in Rome . . ." he muttered urgently.

There was such a thing as taking a resemblance too far. O'Neill rolled his eyes and got to one knee anyway, as did Carter, thinking that the last time O'Neill had genuflected to anyone was . . . probably the last time he'd been in Rome. He declined to bow his head, however.

To the sound of the horns, an elegant couple entered the banquet room, a man clad in gold kilt and breastplate, his eyes outlined in kohl. The veiled woman on his arm was dressed in a tight-fitting dress that looked as if it was made of feathers, a robe in peacock panels, and an elaborate headdress shaped like bird's wings spread and curved around her head. On her forehead, holding the veil in place, she wore a diadem with a uraeus rising from her brow.

The man in gold lifted the woman's veil, took her hand, and displayed her to the bowing multitude.

"Behold your queen!"

She lifted her chin in a haughty gesture, a queen overlooking her subjects. She looked impossibly beautiful, remote, cold.

"Sha're," Daniel whispered.

O'Neill was unable to stop the archaeologist as he lunged to his feet, leaped over the table, running between the kneeling Chulakians. "Sha're, thank God. I thought we'd never—"

But the two were surrounded by protective attendants, and Sha're's eyes flared with an eerie glow. Daniel, seeing it, stumbled to a stop, and O'Neill raised his rifle. There was no recognition in Sha're's eyes. There was nothing human in them either.

"Kneel before your queen," the golden man ordered.

"Sha're, it's *me*!" He tried to move closer, as

if proximity would make a difference. "Sha're!"

The golden one raised his hand. The device wrapped around it flared, the blast knocking Daniel across half the length of the room. O'Neill shouldered his rifle, but Sha're moved in front of the other man, and the colonel hesitated a fraction of a second.

It was a fraction of a second too long. A Serpent guard's staff descended, and the room went black.

CHAPTER TEN

Jackson returned to consciousness and a blinding headache. The shadow leaning over him resolved itself into Carter.

"Sha're?" he mumbled, trying to sit up.

Carter placed a hand on his chest, keeping him down. "Easy, you've been unconscious for hours."

"I saw her—"

"I know," she soothed. "We all did."

"I saw Sha're!" he insisted, as if she hadn't answered. "She was . . ." He took a deep breath. "Where are we?"

"Some sort of holding pen." It was a feeble description of a huge room filled with hundreds of people of all races, all societies. "It happened fast. Apophis sent you across the room, then a guard zapped the colonel. The next thing I remember, we were all here."

Jackson began to sit up, one hand on his aching head. This time Carter let him. He looked around, eyes wide as he realized the implications of the multiplicity of prisoners. "Apophis . . . Apophis. Is that what they called him?"

"You recognize the name?"

"Yeah. Yeah, it's from Egyptian mythology. Ra was the Sun God who ruled the day. Apophis was the Serpent God, Ra's rival; he . . . ruled the night." He blinked, looking up at her. "It's right out of the Book of the Dead. They're *living* it." He swallowed. "What's he done to Sha're? I've got to find her!"

"We can't," Carter said baldly.

"If I can talk to her, I know I can—"

"Daniel, you saw her eyes."

Jackson wasn't willing to accept it. "Maybe it's—it's some kind of drug—"

"These hostiles are parasites," Carter said firmly. "They use human beings as hosts. That's what Ra did."

"I don't believe it." If it was true, if Sha're was— "I'm sorry. I just . . . I just can't."

Someone tall walked toward them out of the crowd, followed by another shadow.

"If there's a way outta here," O'Neill announced to Carter, "I haven't found it yet. But look what I did find." He motioned to the shadow behind him.

"Skaara . . . ?"

The boy rushed to him, hugging him fiercely. "Dani-el! Are you okay?"

Jackson tried to smile. "I think so."

"Welcome back to the land of the living," O'Neill said, finally noticing Jackson was conscious. There was a trace of surprise in his voice. He hunkered down beside the other man to look him over.

"Dani-el, Colonel Jack told me about Sha're."

Jackson looked into the boy's eyes—the eyes that had been so like his sister's before she . . . changed. He couldn't stand it. "Jack, help me. We can find her again—"

"*Daniel.*" The unaccustomed genuine sympathy in O'Neill's voice was worse than any wry comment he could have made. "I'm sorry."

After a moment he added, "Get some rest. By all rights you should be dead."

Jackson turned away and closed his eyes.

Behind him he could hear O'Neill talking to Carter. "You still have the transmitter?" A pause while Carter responded affirmatively. "We may have to destroy it. If we can't find a way to escape, the mission's a failure anyway. We don't want Abadaba or whatever his name is to get his hands on it."

"He still wouldn't know the code," Carter pointed out. "There's half a billion permutations."

"Don't take this personally," O'Neill said sharply, "but . . . *they're way smarter than we are.*"

There was a short silence. Then O'Neill got to his feet, continuing, "Come on, Skaara, let's keep looking for a way out of here."

But there was no sound of movement away. Instead the silence grew deeper, frozen. Daniel opened his eyes.

A Serpent Guard, unmasked, was holding O'Neill's arm in a viselike grip, examining the colonel's watch. He looked very human except for the golden symbol embedded in his forehead: a massive black man, wearing a skullcap, with sharp, inquisitive, dark eyes.

"What is this?" the Guard said. "It is not Goa'uld technology."

O'Neill was making a conscious decision not to try to pull away, basing it on the strong possibility that he would lose his arm if he did so. The decision-making process was nearly derailed by the realization that the man was speaking English, and in a not-unfriendly fashion.

"It's a watch," he said unevenly. "It tells me the time."

He staggered as the Serpent Guard released him abruptly, but held his ground. Jackson watched, wondering at the kind of guts that took.

"Where are you from?" the Serpent Guard asked. He seemed to be impressed as well.

"Earth." O'Neill rubbed his arm surreptitiously.

The information didn't translate, apparently.

"Your word means nothing. Where are you from?"

Daniel sighed. The literal military mind . . . Tapping the man on the leg to get his attention, he sketched the Stargate glyph for *Earth* in the dirt.

The Guard stared at it.

"My name is Daniel, and this is Jack O'N—"

With a violent swipe of his staff the Guard destroyed the drawing in the dirt and walked away.

"Friendly fellow," O'Neill observed.

"What do you think that was about?"

"Maybe he didn't like your drawing." The colonel, in a classic example of unswerving focus on the objective, turned to Skaara. "Come on." And he too walked off, still determined to find the way out.

Kawalsky supposed that it might be colder in Point Barrow, Alaska, in the dead of winter, but it wasn't likely. He had slept uneasily all night, partly because he was afraid that he might not wake up again. He made a mental note to tell Supply about this situation once they got back home. They needed to add warmer blankets to the list.

His team was huddled in lumps around him, covered with frost.

"Warren!" His voice felt as if it were cracking. "Warren!"

The lump next to him stirred.

"The sun is . . . *suns* are . . . coming up. We're gonna be all right."

Suns. Yes. Two of them, framed by the Stargate as they peeked over the horizon. How the hell could it be so cold on a world with *two* suns? he wondered.

Warren brushed his hand against his lips, as if he wasn't sure he could feel them. "We can't go through another night like that, Major."

Kawalsky forced himself to his feet. "I know. The colonel shoulda sent us a radio message by now."

"When do you have to make the decision?" Warren asked. "Whether or not to go back through the Stargate?" Soon, his eyes said. Make it soon.

"That'll be about when hell freezes over," Kawalsky said harshly.

"I think that pretty much describes our current situation," Warren pointed out.

Kawalsky nudged the lump next to him. "We are *not* leaving without the colonel. Rise and shine, boys, it's another fine day on Planet Kawalsky!"

In the briefing room on Earth, Major Bert Samuels reported to his superior. "Sir, the warhead is armed and ready for you to give the word."

Hammond swiveled his chair around, staring down at the sealed disk in the room below. "How much time have they got left?"

"Just under five hours."

"Well, let's keep our fingers off the trigger until the time comes, shall we?"

Samuels saluted.

Every entrance, and there were few enough of them, was guarded. Serpent Guards, faceless in their armored masks, challenged them at every door. O'Neill, Carter, and even Jackson spread out, trying again and again to find a way. Skaara kept close to the man he regarded as his hero.

"Sha're is . . . dead?" he asked tentatively as O'Neill poked at a stone block.

"Yeah," O'Neill answered. Then he thought about it, thought about the cold, remote woman they had seen. "No . . . You know what, Skaara? I don't know."

"We must save her," Skaara protested. "You are a great warrior!" *You're my hero!*

O'Neill flinched. "Look at what we're up against!"

Skaara didn't want to hear it.

Sighing, O'Neill capitulated. "We'll try."

A commotion broke out at the entrance to the room as the huge doors opened. A squad of Serpent Guards cleared a path through the crowd.

Behind them came the dignitaries—in groups of three. Each male-female pair with glowing eyes flanked a third person whose eyes didn't glow but who wore a garment that left the crossed slits in his or her belly exposed. Marching in front of them, clearly their commander, was the Serpent Guard who had earlier wanted to see O'Neill's watch. He alone of the Guards showed a human face.

"Shaka, ha! Kree hol mel, Goa'uld."

Apparently the words made sense to at least some of the crowd; the Serpent Guards herded them into lines, and the people moved into place easily, as if they'd done this many times before. Despite this, it was obvious that they were afraid, not only of the masked guards but even more of the lordly ones those Guards escorted.

"What'd he say?" O'Neill asked Skaara. Carter and Jackson had taken advantage of the commotion to rejoin them.

"They're going to choose," Skaara said.

"Choose what?" Carter demanded.

"Who will become children of the gods."

As Skaara spoke, the end of the procession came in sight—palanquins borne on the shoulders of more Serpent Guards. When they stopped, the canopy was pulled back, to reveal Apophis—and Sha're.

She was wearing different robes this time, loose-fitting solid panels of color, with long silver earrings and an elaborate jeweled headdress. Her eyes, like those of Apophis, were outlined in heavy kohl, and were chillingly empty of emotion.

"Sha're—" Daniel whispered. "Jack, help me. Please."

O'Neill grabbed the other man, preventing him from bodily attacking the Serpent Guards between himself and his wife. "You can't help her, Daniel."

One of the Guards gestured with his staff, indicating O'Neill and his team should join the lines of hundreds of people.

The commander of the Guard stood before them, taking a ceremonial role. *"Benna! Ya wan, ya duru!"* A moment later, he repeated, "Kneel before your masters!"

Hundreds of people fell as one to their knees.

Over their heads, the commander's gaze met O'Neill's. Slowly the colonel knelt, along with Carter. Jackson nearly collapsed beside him. But Skaara continued to stand, staring defiantly at the golden one who had stolen his sister.

"Skaara," O'Neill snapped.

Reluctantly, finally, Skaara knelt too.

The gods with the glowing eyes paced along the lines of kneeling prisoners, assessing them. Apophis and Sha're presided like royalty.

One of the aliens stopped in front of O'Neill, touching his face, turning his head from side to side as if considering. O'Neill stared back, teeth gritted, praying that Skaara, beside him, would have the sense to keep his mouth shut.

A Serpent Guard stood by, staff ready in case any of them was foolish enough to try anything.

The alien rejected him. O'Neill couldn't stop a cold shiver of relief. But it wasn't over; more were coming, and one alien's rejection did not prevent another's choosing.

A female eyed Carter thoughtfully, then turned away.

A pair stopped in front of Daniel, who knelt with his head bowed. The male grabbed him by the hair and pulled his head up, tilting his face to the light.

O'Neill sucked in a breath at the sight of the tears streaming down his friend's face. The aliens, too, seemed impressed; the male wiped a tear away from his victim's cheek, looking over at his mate.

"This one is passionate."

Daniel blinked, staring at them, and then to O'Neill's horror, he spoke: "How much would I remember if you chose *me*—"

"Daniel, what are you doing?" O'Neill whispered frantically. But he knew what Daniel was doing; he could remember his own words as if it were only moments ago: *"I'll never forgive myself. But sometimes I can forget."* Was Daniel seeking forgetfulness, or a way to be closer to Sha're?

"Tell me—!"

The nearest Serpent Guard struck Daniel hard in the face with the end of his staff, and another aimed deliberately at O'Neill. Beyond them, on her golden throne, Sha're watched indifferently.

Daniel spoke now to her. *"Something* of the host must survive . . . ?"

The commander of the Serpent Guards looked away.

The male alien gave Daniel a long look, then shook his head slowly from side to side, almost smiling. *"Nothing."*

His eyes glowed again as he tossed Daniel aside like a rag doll and turned instead to Skaara.

"We choose *him,"* the alien said.

Two Serpent Guards moved forward to take the boy by the arms. Skaara's scream of protest blended with O'Neill's yell, but the colonel's attempt to stop what was happening ended as a Guard struck him down. Skaara continued to scream for O'Neill as he was dragged away.

Apophis stood, Sha're beside him, and as quickly as that the selection process was over, the aliens and their human slaves gathering around him. Apophis looked over the crowd of people and turned to his Commander.

"Kill the rest," he said.

The words didn't make sense to O'Neill for an instant. Then he saw the doors close behind Apophis, Sha're, and the other aliens, and the line of Serpent Guards, staffs charged with energy, moved out into the crowd.

Jumbled images of historical slaughters flashed through O'Neill's mind: Amritsar, Katyn, any concentration camp he cared to name. The death of innocents, the death of the unarmed. He would not, could not allow it. Across the heads of the panicked crowd, he met the eyes of the Serpent Guard commander, the only one of the aliens who had shown any empathy for the plight of the humans.

The rest of the Guards lined up, sliding their weapons into the armed position. The hum of energized staffs rose over the screams and cries.

O'Neill looked the black man in the eye, trying desperately to make some kind of contact as he struggled against the wave of humanity threatening to push him off his feet. The man looked back steadily.

"I can . . . save these people . . . if you help me," O'Neill yelled in a last, frantic appeal.

"Many have said that . . ." the commander answered. The Serpent Guard next to O'Neill grunted with triumph.

Then the energized staff fired.

For a split second O'Neill lay wondering why being dead wasn't any different than dying. Then the body of the Serpent Guard toppled off him.

" . . . but you are the first I believed could do it," the commander added, tossing the weapon to O'Neill.

O'Neill wasted no more time wondering. He energized the weapon and sought a target. As he did so, the commander seized the dead Guard's staff and began to fire as well, over the heads of the screaming mob, blowing holes in the walls behind them, letting the daylight in. As Carter ran to help the crowd through, the commander and O'Neill laid down covering fire, taking out the rest of the startled Serpent Guards.

As the last of the prisoners fled, O'Neill looked at his watch. Time to lockout was growing short. "Hey, c'mon," he snapped.

The commander was dazed, looking over the devastation, at his slaughtered comrades.

"I have nowhere to go," he murmured.

The man had signed his own death warrant, of course, by switching sides.

But by switching sides he'd made himself one of O'Neill's own. "For *this*," the colonel said, "you can stay at *my* place. Let's *go*."

The man looked at him, unsure if the human really meant it, and then tore off his helmet and breastplate, threw them on the dead bodies of the Guards, and followed O'Neill through the wall.

Daniel was standing there, waiting. O'Neill wasn't sure who or what the archaeologist was waiting for, but it didn't matter right now. "You gonna be okay?" he asked sharply.

Daniel nodded, as if numb.

O'Neill turned to the former Serpent commander. "What's your name?"

"Teal'c." The last sound was harsh, hard.

"Teal'c, where will they take Skaara? The boy?"

"To the Stargate. After they've selected hosts for their children, they will return home."

"Not if we get there first," O'Neill said grimly.

CHAPTER ELEVEN

In the Gate room, Hammond and Samuels stood at the bottom of the ramp, looking up at the silent Stargate. Beside them gleamed a metal cylinder with a digital timer.

"Sir, they have just under an hour until the deadline. We should have heard from them by now." Samuels' tone was almost triumphant, as if he had predicted failure all along.

Hammond's gaze never left the Gate, as if he could will it into activation. "A lot can happen in an hour, Major."

58:19.

58:18.

O'Neill glanced at his watch one more time and then back along the line of about forty people he and Carter were leading into the mountains, away from Chulak. "We've got less than an hour," he called to her. "How're we doing?"

"We lost a few when we reached the forest."

Teal'c, following O'Neill, looked warily into the shadows of the surrounding trees. "They will be hunted down and killed. Anyone who does not exist to serve the Gods is their enemy."

"And that makes you—?" O'Neill inquired blandly.

"I am a Jaffa. Bred to serve, that they may live." Teal'c's tone was hard to read. He sounded as if he was reciting a lesson learned long ago—a lesson he hated.

"I don't understand," Daniel said.

Of course not, O'Neill thought. But at least the scientist was asking questions again. O'Neill had never thought he'd live to see the day he was glad when a scientist asked questions.

Teal'c stopped and unstrapped a portion of his armor, then opened his tunic.

A small, translucent white worm stuck its

head out of the crossed slits in Teal'c's belly, twisting and whining like a fretful baby.

"What the hell is that?" O'Neill's staff was pointed unwaveringly at the thing.

Teal'c stared at him. "It is an infant Goa'uld. The larval form of the Gods. I have carried one since I was a child—as all Jaffa carry one."

The worm retracted, and Teal'c closed his tunic.

"Well, get it *outta* there!" O'Neill snapped, shaken.

Teal'c started walking again. "In exchange for carrying the infant Goa'uld until maturity," he said calmly, "a Jaffa receives perfect health and long life. If I was to remove it, I would eventually die."

"If I were you, I'd take my chances!"

Teal'c shook his head, unperturbed, and kept going. "The boy you seek is no longer, you realize."

"I don't wanna hear that," O'Neill informed him. When Teal'c ignored him, he changed the subject. "Why'd you help us?"

The other man chose his words carefully. "You are the first to come along with powers that approach those of the Goa'ulds."

"Powers?"

Teal'c nodded. "You are strong. Perhaps strong enough to destroy them."

Screams from the line of people behind them alerted them to look up into the sky. A large glider soared overhead in the direction of the Stargate.

"Let's go, let's go!" O'Neill was finished with the subject, at least for now. "Skaara's in that thing!"

Teal'c shook his head. "The boy is no longer who he was."

"*I don't wanna hear that*," O'Neill repeated between gritted teeth, picking up his pace.

But Daniel had another thought. "Is it reversible? Can a host become human again?"

Teal'c looked at him with confusion and then surprise. The thought had clearly never occurred to him before. "I am not sure," he admitted.

O'Neill moved up to point, and the line of refugees toiled upward, their breath steaming as the air grew colder. Carter moved up beside Teal'c.

"I should thank you," she said.

At his blank look in response, she added,

"For rescuing us. All of us. If it wasn't for you—"

He understood. "The Goa'ulds are conquerors, nothing more. Not worthy of worship or sacrifice. Not true Gods. Many Jaffa believe they did not even create the Stargates. . . ."

A deafening whine rose in the city. At the same time the earth under their feet began to tremble. Looking up, they saw the alien ship, transformed somehow into a fighter, setting up for a strafing run.

"*Take cover!*" O'Neill yelled. "Stay in the trees!"

The humans screamed as a series of explosions ripped through the foliage, sending chunks of dirt and limbs and leaves into the air. Daniel ran for cover, urging a woman and a very large man dressed in half-cured skins to come with him. The man stood his ground, snarling at the thing in the sky. O'Neill and Teal'c tried to return fire with the staff weapons, but the energy bolts were useless. The ship turned for another run.

At the Stargate, Apophis stood looking down the mountain at the rising smoke, listening to the thin screams of dying human targets, and smiled. Beside him stood a handful of Serpent Guards and the three humans "chosen" at the selection, Skaara among them. The humans listened too, expressionless.

Above him a winged aircraft hovered an instant longer, then vanished toward the line of refugees.

The Stargate opened.

Kawalsky and SG-2 finally obtained their position on the mountainside. Warren shouldered a Stinger, lifting it to bear on the alien craft.

"Hold on . . . hold on," Kawalsky said, scanning the mountain through binoculars.

Below them, Carter yelled to O'Neill. "Colonel, we're sitting ducks here!"

Much as he hated to admit it, the Captain Doctor was right again. "Any ideas?" he asked Teal'c.

Teal'c shook his head.

"Now! *Fire!*" Kawalsky bawled.

The Stinger arced through the air, striking the enemy craft as it streaked low across the mountain. O'Neill grabbed Teal'c's arm and pulled him down into the gravel as the flyer hit the side of the mountain with an ear-shattering explosion. Smoke blossomed from the impact site.

The Earth military yelled in triumph.

Apophis's jaw dropped, and his eyes glowed with insane rage. *"Jaafa, kree Chaaka Ra!"*

In the forest below, Carter stepped out into the open. "Kawalsky?"

"Kawalsky!" O'Neill echoed, rejoicing.

Before the Stargate, two Goa'uld "parents" bowed to Apophis, and with their new "child," the transformed human host, they stepped through the shimmering Gate.

Sha're and Apophis took one more look at the smoke that marked the ruins of their aircraft, and they too stepped through the Gate.

The other "parents" and "children" waited their turn, still watching the mountain burn.

O'Neill and Kawalsky met on a rock outcrop. "Good shot. How many are there?" O'Neill demanded.

"A dozen . . . more. They're going back through the gate. We caught them dialing in the first few symbols from a distance before that ship started shooting and we had to take it out—"

"Skaara?" O'Neill broke in.

Kawalsky swallowed. "He's with them."

Without another word O'Neill started up the last part of the path to the Stargate.

"Sir!" Kawalsky protested, but it did no good.

"We don't have much time before they lock us out!"

O'Neill scrambled, slid, and ran the last part of the way, until he stood before the last group waiting to go through: two Serpent Guards, two Goa'ulds, and the boy he had taken into his heart. The aliens watched him approach, unconcerned.

O'Neill paused. No one was holding Skaara captive; no one was restraining him. He seemed to be with them of his own free will. For the first time he began to wonder if possibly what Teal'c had said was true after all.

The boy smiled, and for a moment O'Neill smiled back, rejoicing, thinking he had made contact after all.

"Skaara?" O'Neill asked tentatively, hope-fully.

Skaara's eyes began to flare.

"No," O'Neill murmured, and aimed his

staff at the Serpent Guards, sure he could still reach the boy if only the others weren't there. But Skaara raised his hand—his hand covered with the Serpent device—and a bolt of energy blasted O'Neill twenty feet into hard gravel.

Shaking his head, dazed, O'Neill watched as Skaara turned away, as he and his companions, the last of the alien group, walked through the shimmering Gate.

And the shimmering stopped, and the Gate closed, and Skaara was gone.

CHAPTER TWELVE

Kawalsky, Jackson, and Carter were the first to make it to O'Neill. Teal'c stood guard, scanning the horizon as if sure trouble wasn't over. Kawalsky eyed him warily, not trusting the alien but taking his cue from the behavior of O'Neill and Carter.

"Did you see the symbols?" Daniel asked desperately.

O'Neill, sick inside, shook his head.

Abruptly, Warren and another man raised the alarm. "Sirs! We got hostiles coming out of the trees!"

They looked down at the treeline and saw alien warriors, armed with energy staffs, emerging from the forest. SG-2 began exchanging fire with them.

"Okay, people, we're going on a little field trip!" Kawalsky said, clapping his hands together. "Better get working on the Stargate, Daniel, we've got company."

Crouching, Jackson ran to the control device, flinching at the sounds of gunfire and energy bolts.

Kawalsky turned to Carter. "Captain, arm your claymores. Warren, Casey, and me'll be the last men out."

O'Neill straightened. "Negative. That's *my* job. Captain, help Daniel. Once you send the signal, I want you to go through and tell them we're bringing company with us."

The captain nodded, grim-faced, and ran to the altar to join Jackson.

A blast from an energy staff came from another direction. From his outlying position Warren called, "We can't hold 'em, sir!"

"Fall back, fall back!" O'Neill returned hoarsely. The party took up defensive positions around the Gate.

Jackson touched a symbol on the altar, and it began to glow.

"Send the signal as soon as it opens, Captain," he said, glancing anxiously over his shoulder at his friends. The earth began to tremble once more.

The Gate shimmered.

Back in Earth's control room, Hammond paced, watching the clock tick toward zero, unwilling to cheat his men out of a single second of time. A technician called out to him, "General, our Gate is spinning up—still no signal—"

"Sir," Samuels said urgently.

Hammond took a deep breath, glancing at Samuels, who was shaking his head. "All right. Seal it off."

"Wait! There it is! A wormhole has just been set up on the other side. . . . We have the code! Verified!"

"Belay that last order!" Hammond roared. "Squad, stand by!"

Frantically, Jackson punched in the last digits of the transmitter code. "Is it working?" he asked. A bolt of energy sizzled over his head.

"Let's hope so," the captain answered, pressing the transmitter button firmly. All around them the battle continued, pressing ever closer. Dirt fountained within arm's reach as another energy bolt just missed its target. Carter wormed her way forward, got to her feet, and turned to give Jackson a last message. "Give me a few seconds, then start sending them through!"

Realizing their escape route was open at last, O'Neill yelled, "Hit the claymores!"

Kawalsky turned the detonator. A series of explosions caught a new skirmish line of Chulak warriors, sending pieces of them flying.

Daniel stood by the Gate, waving the refugees through as fast as possible.

"Daniel, if we can't hold 'em, you're gonna have to go through and tell 'em to close the door!" O'Neill shouted.

Jackson sniffled—or perhaps snorted in derision—and kept pushing the refugees through.

They were surrounded now. Kawalsky, Warren, and O'Neill were fighting behind the stone structure of the Gate itself. Aiming didn't matter anymore; no matter where they pointed a gun there was a target waiting.

Next to O'Neill, the former prisoner clad in half-cured skins was throwing rocks at the advancing battle line. O'Neill did a double-take and snatched up an M-16. "Here! Use this!"

The man looked down at the weapon, grunted, and threw the thing like a javelin. It hit a Chulak dead on, knocking him down.

Whatever worked. O'Neill patted the man on the arm. "Good!"

In the Gate room, Carter herded refugees to the bottom of the ramp, fending off armed security's unwavering rifles and answering Hammond's unwavering questions. Both captain and general glanced anxiously, repeatedly, at each new arrival through the Gate.

The last of the refugees, except the primitive who had taken up arms—or rocks—had passed through the Gate. "That's it!" Daniel yelled.

"You go!" O'Neill was still firing.

Jackson gave him a long look and then stepped through.

"Casey, Warren! Go!"

Casey and Warren fired their last shots and turned to run for the Gate. They were almost there when Casey fell with a cry right beside the control panel. Warren stopped to help him.

"Warren! Leave him!"

Anguished, Warren obeyed.

One of the Chulak warriors managed to evade fire and make it to the control panel, within touching distance of Kawalsky. O'Neill caught sight of him as the alien started to place his hand on the controls, and aimed.

The primitive beside him snarled and rushed, taking the warrior around the waist. The alien screamed as ribs snapped.

"Cover me!" Kawalsky yelled, and rose to his feet to race for Casey.

Something white hissed from the Serpent Guard as he died under the primitive's savage embrace. Kawalsky shuddered but moved, picking up the wounded man, and ran for the Gate.

The primitive dropped the dead warrior and raised his fists to the sky, screaming in triumph and revenge. As he did so, a dozen energy bolts converged on him.

O'Neill and Teal'c realized that they were the last ones left. Covering each other, firing frantically, they dove through the Stargate.

"Now!" Carter screamed. *Lock it up!*

The iris closed, scissoring the head of a Chulak who had followed too close. The serpent helmet dropped onto the ramp, rolling between O'Neill and Teal'c. A wave of delirious refugees surrounded the colonel, weeping, hugging him. Teal'c remained at the top of the ramp alone.

"Colonel O'Neill," Hammond said in measured tones, studying the renegade Serpent Guard, "care to explain?"

"We can use the Stargate to send them home," Carter spoke up, referring to the refugees.

"What's *he* doing here?" The general was not to be swayed by distractions.

"This," panted the colonel, "is Teal'c. He can help us."

Hammond had recognized the former commander. "Do you know *what* he is, Colonel?"

O'Neill drew a deep breath and looked his commanding officer square in the eye. "Yes, sir. He's the man who saved our lives. And if you accept my recommendation, he'll join SG-1."

To give Hammond credit, he did not recommend O'Neill for a Section Eight then and there. Instead he said in measured tones, "That decision may not be up to you."

The tension of the moment was broken by a team of medics rushing in. Kawalsky stole a moment from the CPR he was rendering to Casey. "C'mon, c'mon, c'mon!"

As the medics moved in, Kawalsky stepped back. O'Neill and Hammond, having declared a temporary truce, went down the ramp.

Kawalsky winced suddenly, slumping against the wall, rolling his head. Then he straightened up again as if nothing had happened.

One of the medics looked up at the general, shaking his head, as the others kept going: "One, two, three, four, five! One, two, three, four, five!"

"Keep trying!" Warren beseeched them.

Hammond took his arm. "He's gone, son."

The medics lay Casey on a stretcher, covering his face with a sheet, and Warren broke down in sobs.

"Major Kawalsky?" Hammond went on.

Kawalsky stepped away from the wall. "Sir!"

"Colonel O'Neill, Major Kawalsky, the sure-to-be-very-interesting debriefing for SG units one and two will be at 0730."

"Yes, sir," Kawalsky and O'Neill chorused.

Samuels stepped forward, clapping his hands for attention. "All right. Let's work on getting these people home where they belong."

O'Neill studied his fellow team leader. "Kawalsky . . . you okay?"

Kawalsky nodded. O'Neill decided to leave the other man alone; everyone reacted differently to the letdown after battle. If Kawalsky wanted to be left alone, fine.

Daniel Jackson was finding loneliness hard to bear. O'Neill shared the feeling, moving to stand beside him as he stared at the Stargate.

"She's out there somewhere, Jack," the young man said.

"I know she is," O'Neill said softly. "So's Skaara."

"What do we do?" he said miserably.

"Find them," came the answer, inflexible, determined. He slapped the other man on the shoulder.

The refugees lined up to pass on their knowledge of their home coordinates to the technicians, and Carter and Teal'c joined O'Neill and Jackson to watch the operation of the Stargate, the alien technology within human reach but as yet outside their grasp. It represented endless new possibilities, new adventures, new hope.

Behind them Kawalsky watched too as the gate shimmered and refocused. And he too saw new possibilities . . .

. . . with eyes that glowed.

THE STARGATE SERIES
by Ashley McConnell

STARGATE SG-1
0-451-45726-9

The Stargate has been breached by the serpent
god Apophis. Only Colonel Jack O'Neill
possesses the courage to lead an elite group to
stop Apophis before she destroys the alternate
universe.

Look for the rest of the Stargate series,
coming soon from Roc:

The Price You Pay
0-451-45726-9

The First Ammendment
0-451-45777-3

The Morpheus Factor
0-451-45816-8

Available wherever books are sold or at
www.penguin.com

Penguin Group (USA) Inc. Online

What will you be reading tomorrow?

Tom Clancy, Patricia Cornwell, W.E.B. Griffin,
Nora Roberts, William Gibson, Robin Cook,
Brian Jacques, Catherine Coulter, Stephen King,
Dean Koontz, Ken Follett, Clive Cussler,
Eric Jerome Dickey, John Sandford,
Terry McMillan...

You'll find them all at
http://www.penguin.com

*Read excerpts and newsletters,
find tour schedules, and enter contests.*

Subscribe to Penguin Group (USA) Inc. Newsletters
and get an exclusive inside look
at exciting new titles and the authors you love
long before everyone else does.

PENGUIN GROUP (USA) INC. NEWS
http://www.penguin.com/news